Up to the time that her sister Eileen had married, Anne Veigh had lived in the shadow of Eileen's more striking, more vivacious beauty. The older girl's marriage had taken her away from the small Southern city where the Veighs lived, and had also definitely removed her from the orbit of Kenny, who had once loved Eileen and whom Anne had always loved.

As Anne's quiet charm ripened with maturity, Kenny realized that she too had a great deal to offer a man, and they became engaged. Anne floated on roseate clouds of bliss.

Then Eileen announced that she was coming home for a visit. And her sister was once more beset by doubts concerning both her own attractiveness and the depth of Kenny's affection for her.

BELIEVE IN LOVE

BELIEVE IN LOVE

by

FERN SHEPARD

PRESTIGE BOOKS
NEW YORK, NEW YORK

Prestige Books, Inc.
18 East 41st Street, New York, New York 10017
Printed in the United States of America

BELIEVE IN LOVE

CHAPTER 1

Her mother broke the news when Anne came down to breakfast. "What do you think, darling?" Nellie Veigh said, fluttering her pretty ringed fingers over the letter she had just finished reading. "Eileen is coming home. She and Bob are not getting along."

For a moment Anne couldn't say a single solitary word.

She felt exactly as if someone had handed her a prettily wrapped package containing an unexploded bombshell. She was not aware of dipping her spoon into the piece of ice cold melon which was waiting at her plate, nor did she actually taste her first sip or two of coffee.

Eileen was coming home! And what did that mean?

Kenny is mine. Instinctively her mind shaped the words. They were, however, the expression of a fear, not a certainty. The vague, unadmitted fear which her heart had always known.

"Of course," Nellie was continuing, "I've never approved of such disagreements between married couples, but there are exceptions to all rules. Furthermore, I never did feel that Bob Thompson—" With a vague sigh, she left the sentence hanging in mid-air. Anne picked it up.

"What's the matter with Bob?" She knew that the words sounded curt, that she was rushing to Bob's defense without knowing any of the details. But there was this sudden fear in her and she had not had time to learn to cope with it. She knew that her fear was part and parcel of her jealousy of Eileen. Therefore her sympathies were with Bob. Anyway, Bob was all right— an ambitious, steady-going, hard working young engineer who had showed quite plainly that he adored the ground that Eileen walked on. It would take a lot of convincing to make Anne believe that Bob was the one who had failed in the marriage.

She said, spooning sugar into a second cup of coffee: "You never believed that anyone was good enough for Eileen, Mother." And she couldn't keep the bitterness out of her next words. "You didn't even think that Kenny was good enough for her. But when Kenny fell in love with me, you seemed to think that I was a lucky girl."

Her mother patted the carefully set waves of snowy white hair which gave the lie to her youthful and still pretty face. Her wide, surprisingly alert blue eyes flashed annoyance. "I'm surprised at you, Anne. If your sister is unhappy, she's doing exactly the right thing to come right straight home where she belongs. And as for Bob, I don't recall ever having said that he wasn't good enough for Eileen. If he had succeeded in making her happy, I'd be the last one to say a word against him. But she is miserably unhappy, and I think it's partly because Bob is a little too crude to understand Eileen's sensitive make-up."

Anne had to smile to herself. Eileen's "sensitive make-up" was something she'd been having impressed on her ever since she'd been old enough to understand what the words meant. Eileen was spoiled and pampered and selfish, because her mother had made her that way. That's what Eileen's "sensitive make-up" amounted to. If that was being catty, then Anne was catty and had no apologies to make for it. It wasn't that she really disliked her sister—four years older than herself—who had always been considered the beauty of the family. But she felt that to like a person, you needn't harbor a lot of foolish illusions about them.

Anne had no illusions whatever about Eileen. However, her mother, who doted on Eileen, had nothing else but. That was about what it got down to.

"What I did say at the time," Nellie was explaining, "was that I believed Eileen could have done better for herself if she had been willing to wait. I just never saw a girl who had so many chances to marry. Almost every man who came along seemed to fall in love with her, and I begged and pleaded with her not to be in such a hurry.

I remember saying to her—we were sitting here right at this same kitchen table where you and I are sitting now—'Eileen, if you go rushing into this marriage without taking more time to think it over, you mark my words, the day will come when you'll regret it.'"

Anne didn't need to be reminded. How well she remembered the arguments, tearful and pleading, on her mother's part. Eileen was mostly defiant and didn't want to hear a word of it. "I love Bob and I'm going to marry him before he goes off to war, and nobody can stop me," was what she kept repeating. It had gone on for a solid week. Anne remembered that Saturday night when Eileen came home from a dance, her dark eyes starry, her mouth tremulous with emotional excitement, to announce that she and Bob Thompson were engaged. And then the following Saturday they were married, very quietly, in the front parlor of the rambling old house where three generations of Veigh women had been born and grown up and fallen in love and married.

In this small, typically southern town, where a girl just had to be born with some claim to beauty and charm if she wanted to get ahead, the beauty of the "Veigh women" was traditional. Oldtimers, in describing them to newcomers, would say: "The Veigh women are always beauties." And then they would say, or had said until Eileen got married and left town, "Now you take Eileen Veigh. Did you ever see such a raving beauty?"

The wedding, although quiet, with only the family and closest friends in attendance, had been lovely. The gleam of lighted candles threw a sheen over the white satin altar in the old-fashioned bay window. The pungent fragrance of early spring roses filled the air. Bob looked so handsome in his uniform with the brand new silver bars on his shoulders, and so tall and proud as he waited there near the altar for Eileen to join him. Eileen, in white satin, her bouquet of long-stemmed roses cradled in her arm, looked beautiful and far more exotic and excitingly lovely than any mere angel ever looked.

She wore no veil, and the glossy waves of her chestnut dark hair shone with a coppery gleam.

As she had come slowly into the room on Uncle Ned's arm, her eyes, large and always darkly luminous, had seemed to blaze with happiness and suppressed excitement. Here was no shy, reluctant, timid bride. Here was a gorgeous girl, thrilling to all the wonder of youth and love and the awareness of her own beauty, impatient to catch up with the happiness that was waiting for her and to drink deeply and richly of it.

Anne, only sixteen at the time, had been her sister's only attendant. She had worn pale blue net over deeper blue taffeta, and as one or two people said afterwards, "Anne looked real sweet, too." But Anne, of course, couldn't hold a candle to Eileen for looks. And never would.

Sometimes, when she thought about it, Anne would feel a little ashamed that the only emotion she had felt that day was a sense of great relief. She had stood there by the altar, holding Eileen's bouquet while her sister knelt by Bob's side. She had known, without needing to look, that her mother was crying softly. And she had known that Kenny Wilcox, Eileen's recently discarded fiancé, was standing at the back of the room, his face set and grim. If there were no tears in his eyes, they were in his heart.

There had been others with wet eyes—Aunt Molly Graham for one—and with a sense of loneliness in their hearts, because while they rejoiced in Eileen's happiness, they wept over their own loss of her. She was going away with her man, to make her own home, to build her own life as a wife and, in time, a mother. She would be back on visits, but she would never really belong to them again, and for this they sorrowed.

All except Anne! With Eileen gone, now maybe I'll have a chance, she had thought. It wasn't exactly a thing to be proud of, to look back and remember that as your chief reaction to your only sister's marriage.

Glad to get rid of her sister, to get her out of the house, out of the town? Well, that was hardly a fair way to put it. At least Anne didn't think so. But was there anything shameful about being sick and tired of being so overshadowed by Eileen's beauty and popularity? How she hated her sister's very clever way of drawing all attention to herself and keeping it there so that people scarcely seemed to notice that Anne was even alive!

She came back out of her brief reverie to hear her mother saying the words which, in Anne's opinion, were certainly uncalled for. If she hadn't known her mother so well, Anne could have taken them for intentional cruelty. But she knew better. There was no cruelty or even unkindness in Nellie's gentle nature. It was simply that where her favorite daughter was concerned, she seemed to have a completely blind spot as to the feelings of others. So now she said:

"I can't help but wish sometimes that Eileen had never broken off with Kenny. She was crazy enough about him at one time, and now that he's doing so well as a doctor, I half blame myself for discouraging that match. But Kenny hadn't finished college at the time, and as a youngster he was such a quiet boy, I just didn't know if he'd ever amount to much. If I had realized—"

Anne had a wild desire to scream or to smash something. By a supreme effort of will she kept her voice perfectly controlled. "You seem to forget, Mother, that Kenny and I are engaged. Do you think it's kind to talk as if Kenny were only marrying me because he couldn't get Eileen?"

"I'm sorry, dear," her mother said quickly. "I shouldn't have said that. I just didn't think. Five years is a long time, and of course you are the one Kenny wants now. But I just couldn't help remembering how broken up he seemed at Eileen's wedding."

There was a wide streak of cruelty in Eileen's nature, or was it being unfair to think of it that way? Perhaps it had been only the selfish vanity of a still adolescent girl which had made Eileen insist upon inviting Kenny to her wedding, after having jilted him only a few short weeks before.

Even her mother, at the time, had questioned the good taste of that invitation. "After all, dear, we're having very few outside the family. And Kenny must feel terribly broken up about your throwing him over. It scarcely seems necessary to fling your marriage to another man in his face."

But Eileen had insisted. "I want Kenny at my wedding, Mother. After all, he's one of my oldest friends and we've been so close."

"Yes. Eileen and I were very close. I loved her very dearly. It's hard for me to remember back to when I wasn't in love with Eileen. It's pretty hard for me to get used to the idea that she's married another man and gone away with him."

That had been Kenny talking. Several hours after Eileen was married. After the festivities were over, and Eileen and Bob had left for their week-end honeymoon in a secluded spot in the Virginia Blue Ridge mountains, Anne and Kenny had slipped out of the house to take a walk together.

They had always been good friends, although Kenny, at twenty-two, looked upon Anne, six years younger, as still a child. And his manner toward her was that of an older brother. That night, for the first time, he had treated her almost as an equal in years and experience. But that, Anne had suspected, was because he was scarcely aware of her as a person. His thoughts turned in upon his own unhappiness, he was scarcely aware of anything except that he had loved Eileen and lost her. And that he was torn and racked and hurting with emotions that refused to accept the facts as they were.

"But I guess I'll get over it," he had said finally, with a ghost of a smile. "I'm not the first guy to lose the girl he wanted. And if all those other guys got over it in time, I guess I will too." Yet he hadn't sounded as if he really believed what he said.

With some vague idea of cheering him up, Anne had told him: "You make me sick, Kenny Wilcox. Going around sounding as if you'd lost your last friend. If I were a man, and a girl gave me the kind of a dirty deal that Eileen gave you, I wouldn't give her a second thought. And if I did, I'd just hate myself for being such a weak, silly, spineless, love-sick idiot."

Somewhat intrigued by this outburst, Kenny had grinned at her. He had really grinned, for the first time in days. "What would you do, Miss
You just tell me that. If you were a man, Miss Smarty, and this happened to you, what would you do?"

"I'd go right out and find somebody else to fall in love with, that's what I'd do."

An idea worth some thought, Kenny had agreed promptly. Then he had given Anne a curious look and he had said a curious thing: "But you're still too young, Anne. That's the whole trouble. You're still too young."

She had given him a look out of startled eyes. "What do you mean, I'm too young?"

"Just what I say, honey. If I can't have Eileen, you're my next best bet. But you're only sixteen. I'll tell you what, Anne. You hurry up and grow up a few more years. When you are about twenty, we'll talk this thing over again."

Kenny had been a little late living up to that promise. He had waited until her twenty-first birthday to ask Anne to marry him. That had been a little over a month ago.

"It was that terrible war," Nellie was saying, just as she'd said at the time of Eileen's marriage and, never really reconciled, had reiterated a thousand times since.

Having heard it so often, Anne knew that little refrain by heart: Wars always led to so many impulsive marriages that were doomed from their very inception, and that's what had happened to Eileen. Her head had been completely turned by so much attention from the officers in that training camp nearby. There had been so many men falling madly in love with her. Remember that Christmas Eve dance at the Officers' Club when she had been voted the most beautiful girl in Virginia, and received three proposals of marriage that very same night?

"So what?" Anne wanted to scream.

Nellie never wearied of living over Eileen's little triumphs and Anne had been sick of hearing about them from the very start. Five years of repetition. It was like nagging at a nerve worn raw. Eileen was so popular— Eileen had so many admirers—Eileen was so beautiful— Eileen, Eileen, Eileen.

What girl wouldn't be sick of it?

Especially when it was impossible to miss the not too well hidden implication: What a pity you can't be the popular beauty your sister was! Oh, Nellie had never said that in so many words. But Anne knew! She knew that it was in her mother's mind, and that most of the town probably agreed with her.

Her breakfast finished, Anne saw no point in prolonging the conversation. It was already after nine. Nellie, every inch the southern lady complete with Virginia accent, soft pretty hands that disliked menial work, and an inborn conviction that a real lady shouldn't go running off to an office at the stroke of nine, had never taken Anne's job as secretary to a lawyer very seriously.

But Anne took it seriously, and it was time for her to be getting off. Her mother, she knew, would be perfectly willing to keep her sitting here the whole morning, recalling Eileen's past triumphs, holding post-mortems over the marriage which should never have been.

Anne folded the heavy linen napkin, smiling to herself as she did so. It had taken literally years to persuade Nellie to breakfast in this sunny kitchen nook, deserting the large and somewhat dismal dining room for all meals except dinner. But to fall so low as to use paper napkins, which could be so easily crumpled and discarded, *never*. There was, she always contended, something definitely common—at any rate, unpleasantly suggestive of a lack of sensitivity—about paper napkins. For outdoor picnics, yes. But to be used on her own lovely table that was invariably set, even in the kitchen, with the family sterling and the crystal goblets?

Oh, no. Nellie would flinch, with an expression faintly resembling pain, at the very thought.

And if her mother was so completely unrealistic about a little thing like paper napkins, how could anyone expect her to be realistic about Eileen, who, since father's death nearly eleven years ago, had been the apple of Nellie's eye.

Anne thought, a little ashamed of her own suppressed resentments: I shouldn't get upset because mother adores Eileen the way she does. Nellie Veigh, by nature, was drawn to beauty and daintiness. Even in the year 1950, her imagined ideal girl was the old-fashioned southern belle—exquisitely beautiful, gay, charming, thoughtless of the more serious things of life. In short, a breathtaking beauty to whom the world was a collection of admirers swarming around her, like moths to a flame. And Eileen was just such a person.

While as for herself, Anne thought, quite honestly, I'm just a quiet, mousy little person with no looks to speak of. Never in a thousand years would it occur to anyone to vote her a Virginia beauty. And as for receiving three proposals of marriage in an evening, it had taken twenty-one years and a lot of praying and hoping for her to get just one proposal of marriage! A thought which amused her momentarily, until she remembered that it was Eileen whom Kenny had loved first.

. He had admitted to Anne, no longer ago than the night when he asked her to marry him, that when Eileen jilted him it had nearly killed him.

Grinning ruefully: "I was like the guy in that corny old song: *A Fool There Was.* Couldn't eat, couldn't sleep, dreamed about the gal when I did sleep, and actually gave a lot of concentrated thought to killing myself. Oh, it hit me hard, all right, but finally I grew up and got to be a big boy. Finally I got over it."

Had he gotten over it?

Anne knew now, facing the prospect of Eileen's return, that she had never been really sure. And when Eileen came back and indicated that her marriage was not going smoothly, what would happen?

How would Kenny feel when he saw her again, knowing that maybe it still was not too late? The very thought was like a clammy hand of fear laid on her heart.

And out of the fear, the angry resentment spurted up again, unbidden, irrepressible, and it made her eyes hard and unsympathetic as she pushed back her chair and heard her mother still talking about that other war, the parade of Eileen's triumphs: "I never could understand what possessed her to settle on Bob Thompson when she had so many other chances. She was the most popular girl in this town. It was a rare thing when there wasn't some young officer waiting in the parlor for her. Or out on the front porch. Often as not, there would be three or four of them waiting together, and all looking daggers at each other. The flowers used to simply pour in. And candy! Just pounds and pounds and pounds of it. I used to have to give it away to the neighbors. And when one of the boys would be transferred, out west or wherever, then the telegrams would start coming. And the long distance phone ringing."

"I'm sick of it! Do you hear me, Mother? I'm sick and tired and fed up with hearing about all the men who were in love with Eileen during the last war. I'm sick of hearing about Eileen's beauty and Eileen's popularity. I'm just sick of hearing about Eileen, period."

Anne stood up, and her eyes blazed with the stormy resentment, partly a sense of injustice, which had been smoldering in her for years. Years? For practically all of her life. For since she was a toddling baby just beginning to understand words, there had never been a time when the beauty of her older sister was not being constantly thrown up to her.

It had been a long time ago—she could have been no more than seven or eight at the time, but she could still remember, as clearly as if it were yesterday—that she had heard a low-spoken conversation between her mother and father. Anne had stood, her ear pressed to the closed folding doors between the front and back parlors, and those words, idly spoken, had taken root in her young brain like tough, ugly, indestructible weeds.

"Anne is such a plain child compared with Eileen. Honestly, Tom, no one would take them for sisters. Such a pity! Life is so much easier for a girl with beauty."

"I wouldn't be so sure about Anne's plainness, Nellie." Even when she was a baby, her daddy had been the one whom Anne adored. Right then, her heart seemed about to burst with gratitude as well as tenderness for him. For with those words he seemed to offer her a fighting chance at life and happiness, the chance at her woman's birthright, of which her mother would have robbed her in the space of a breath.

"There's something about Anne's face. She will never possess the more obvious kind of good looks which hit you in the eye, but there is more than one kind of beauty, Nellie. Anne's face has a kind of spiritual quality, and as she grows older I think it will intensify. I daresay there will be many who will miss it altogether, but I also predict there will be those who will consider her the more beautiful of the two girls.

"What's more," he had added, after a moment's thought, "there's a lot more to our little Anne than mere superficial prettiness. You mark my words, we'll be proud of that little girl some day."

Well, Tom Veigh hadn't lived to find out whether he'd have reason to be especially proud of his Anne or not. He'd gone before his time—the victim of one of those careless accidents which never should have happened. But to Anne, the one who had been inconsolable in her young grief and her first experience with deep sorrow, he would always be the human being she had loved most dearly. And those words he had spoken, way back in the past, had helped to keep him alive in her heart.

Whenever she felt hurt, or put upon by some favoritism shown Eileen, she would remember her father's deep love for her, his many little manifestations of affection. He had been a demonstrative man, never ashamed of showing love and tenderness. And she would remember the words he had said that day: "There will be those who will consider Anne very beautiful."

Well, he had been wrong about that. No one had ever called her beautiful, nor had she ever accomplished anything to make anyone especially proud of her.

She seemed to have remained much what she had been

as a little girl—quiet, unobtrusive, never one to push herself, well liked by everyone in town, especially by older people, because she always tried to be thoughtful and considerate of others. Alex Brooks said she was the best secretary he had ever had.

So her father had been wrong, after all. Except that he had made her feel beautiful, important and wanted as no one else had ever done. When things were hard, when she was hurt, her mind would rush to her memories of him and it was like touching a loving, bolstering hand.

There had been many a time when, just thinking of him and of his tenderness, she had been able to force back angry, rebellious, bitter words which beat at her to be spoken. But he was no help now.

Now, for the very first time, as she stood there facing her mother's startled, bewildered eyes, she allowed the full, frantic torrent of her rebellious spirit to possess her and to flow out of her in words she should have said years ago.

Her hands gripped the back of her chair and her head was flung a little back. "All my life I've had Eileen's looks flung in my face. Do you remember the very first words you ever taught me to say, Mother? Do you? My *sister Eileen is beautiful.* You made me say it over and over and over and over. Remember, Mother?

"I learned it in the cradle, from you. Later on, I had to listen to it everywhere I turned. What a beautiful girl your sister is. Eileen looked beautiful as an angel on the Sunday she took her first communion. Eileen, such a beautiful girl graduate. Eileen, the loveliest bride you ever saw. Eileen—what a beautiful mother she will make, a regular madonna. Only Eileen fooled them there. Eileen isn't ready to be a mother. She isn't even ready to be a wife. She misses the excitement of being dated and admired by a different worshipping male each night. She misses the candy and the flowers and the telephone calls and the attention she received as a glamour girl."

She flung the words straight in her mother's face. Mrs. Veigh had turned pale. She seemed to be struggling between amazement at Anne's unexpected outburst and hurt shock that such unkind things should be said about Eileen.

"Oh, I know you'll hate me for saying this, Mother. But I know Eileen better than you do. You don't know her at all. You simply worship at her shrine. I say that Eileen is a self-centered creature who simply must be admired by every man she comes in contact with. As a wife, she can't expect to have men swooning at her feet. And she's bored now without it. That's the reason she's breaking up with Bob.

"Don't tell me that Bob has been unkind and cruel to her, because I don't believe a word of it. Bob is the gentlest soul who ever lived. He couldn't be unkind to a girl even if he hated her, and he worshipped Eileen.

You know it.

"Eileen is coming home for just one reason. Married life provides her with but one admirer and Eileen still hasn't lost her yen to be the belle of the ball!"

Suddenly she was like a clock that had run down. Her outburst was over as abruptly as it had started. She looked at her mother who sat, tight-lipped, shocked, still too bewildered to think what to say. "I'm sorry, Mother." Her apology was little more than a whisper.

Then she turned and walked out of the kitchen.

She went up to her bedroom. She would have to bathe her eyes and put on fresh lipstick before she went to the office. She stood for a moment before her dressing table mirror.

The girl who looked back at her, if not spectacularly beautiful, had a very real charm that was singularly her own. Her hair was an off shade of gold, and her eyes, gravely thoughtful, were such a deep, shining blue that they were often taken for black. Her lips were wide and sweetly curved, and her smile was warm and genuine. A startling beauty? No. In all honesty, she wasn't.

But Tom Veigh had been right, years ago, when he had said that Anne's face possessed some peculiar arresting quality of loveliness. It was an elusive quality, not to be measured in terms of the color of her eyes nor the shape of her nose. But it was a loveliness that came from something deep within her. A clean, delicate, glowing type of beauty that was covered by Anne's shyness and lack of confidence. But some day it would burst forth and she would emerge into a truly beautiful girl.

However, few people saw any of this in Anne, and certainly she saw none of it in herself. She had never looked more plain to herself than she did at that moment. She studied herself briefly and without enthusiasm, reddened her lips, straightened her white silk blouse, and turned away from the mirror.

Already she was regretting her impulsive outburst. But every word that I said was true, she reminded herself. Or was it? Had she said less than the truth, or more? Quickly her uncertain mind threw up the doubts that had been waiting right along to hound her. Ten days ago she had written Eileen about her engagement to Kenny. Could that be the thing that was bringing Eileen back with such alarming suddenness?

Was she breaking up with Bob, rushing home with her marriage in ruins behind her, to get Kenny back again before it was too late? Or to try to?

And if it were that? What about Kenny? Would he be willing to be drawn back into the pretty web she would try to weave? Had he ever really gotten over the girl whom he had loved so deeply and who, in jilting him, had made him suffer so much?

"Oh, I'm over Eileen." Any number of times he had reassured Anne on that point. "Why, it's hard for me to remember exactly what she looked like. Isn't that enough proof? Every guy has to have a girl in his past—the first girl he fell for—and that's what Eileen means to me. That's all she means to me, believe me. I hardly ever think about her any more, and when I do, it's just to recall some silly thing that happened between us. No, darling, you're my girl now. You're the girl in my present, the only girl I want in my future. Isn't that good enough to suit you?"

Anne went slowly down the curved stairway, her hand trailing the lovely old mahogany banister railing. Her eyes were wide and far away. Oh, that was good enough, surely: to be the girl in Kenny's present and future was plenty good enough—if only it were true! But was it?

How could Kenny himself know what was true? How could he possibly know what he would feel, what long-buried emotions might rush to quick and demanding life when he saw Eileen again?

But I'll know, Anne thought. I'll know the minute I see him look at her. Then, as she reached the lower hallway, the phone rang.

"I'll answer it," Anne called to her mother. The phone alcove, partially hidden under the stairway, had once been a large closet. As Anne walked back to it, she knew who would be calling. She knew what she was going to hear, before she ever lifted the receiver from its cradle.

"Anne? Ken speaking."

Ken speaking! The very formality of those words sent a shiver of foreboding through her. As if she wouldn't be expected to recognize the voice of the boy she had known her whole life—the voice of the man she still hoped she was going to marry.

"Well—" a thread of mockery appeared in her tone—"aren't we formal this morning. It's a wonder you wouldn't inform me it was Dr. Wilcox calling."

She heard his laugh. The quick, deeply soft, throaty laugh which did things to her heart and always had. "I'm talking from the phone in the waiting room, and the room is crowded with patients. I was hoping I'd catch you before you left for the office. Look, Anne, how about lunch together?"

"Something important?" Anne asked quickly. A natural question, since Kenny made a rule of avoiding luncheon engagements. He never quite knew when he could get away from his offices which were, in a very small way, a clinic. Nor could he ever tell in advance what emergency calls might come up.

Then, with a quick tightening of her throat, Anne heard him laugh again. And this time was it tinged with embarrassment? Or was that simply her imagination playing tricks on her? She thought not.

"Well, I suppose you might say it is important. Fact is, I just had a letter from Eileen. Quite a surprise. I wanted to talk it over with you."

Anne's voice came quiet, under perfect control.

"Okay, Kenny. I'll meet you at one o'clock sharp. In front of Gordon's Grill? Fine. Be seeing you, darling."

She cradled the phone. She let her hands fall, crossed, in her lap. Then, for a solid three minutes, she sat staring at nothing at all.

CHAPTER 2

Alex Brooks, at thirty-eight, was the dark, dashing, definitely he-man type, and still looked in his very early thirties. He was generally regarded as the most eligible bachelor in Hillview. Unfortunately, from every standpoint but his own, he was also the most elusive one.

"I am waiting," Alex would say, grinning, "for my ideal girl to come along." Pinned down, he would elaborate, still in that humorous tone.

His ideal must excel all others in beauty, charm, intellect, and character. She must not only be able to wear clothes like a *Vogue* model but also make apple pies the way his mother used to make them.

Since, obviously, no such paragon of perfection exsted anywhere outs of his imagination, it was simply another way of saying that Alex had no intention of marrying at all.

Still, the mothers of Hillview's marriageable daughters remained hopeful. They had been so for nearly ten years, ever since Alice Jordan, the girl whom Alex had loved deeply, had been taken suddenly ill and died. It all happened just one short week before the day set for their wedding. "You'd be so much better off with a wife, Alex," they said. It must be hard on his digestion, eating in restaurants all the time. And certainly lonely, going to bed and sleeping and getting up mornings in that apartment, all by himself.

It always made him chuckle quietly to himself to think about how the ambitious mamas of as yet unspoken for daughters worried about his digestion and his loneliness. Both of which, he would always assure them, were holding up beautifully.

He saw through their little tricks and schemes and arguments, and was amused by them. When he was invited out to dinner, and told that "dear little Marjorie insisted upon cooking every bit of this dinner with her own hands," Alex knew perfectly well that dear Marjorie's qualifications as a wife and cook were being paraded for his benefit. And the same held true when he called to escort Marjorie to a dance, and was told by her mama: "Doesn't my little girl look lovely in that frock? And just imagine! She made every stitch of it by herself. Such a thrifty, practical-minded child. As she said to me, 'Mama, whatever is the sense in my paying a lot of money to one of those old stores for a formal when I can make one twice as pretty for myself for next to nothing?' "

Really, quite out of the ordinary, this Marjorie! Doubtful, very doubtful, if a man would ever find her like again. And there were a dozen or more girls like Marjorie in town. And more coming along each year. Strange, indeed, that Alex never took it into his head to settle on one of them. And downright provoking, too. He was practically everything that the average mother dreams of in a husband for her daughter: inherited money, in addition to the good, solid income he was earning from his practice; recognition as an excellent lawyer who, if he chose, could easily get into politics and make a name for himself.

Whereas the mamas were taken by Alex's desirability from an economic standpoint, the daughters went all out for his good looks and charm. He was dark-eyed, definitely handsome, with the kind of a flashing smile that teen-aged girls dream about. And he had that certain something in his voice when he spoke a girl's name that made her imagine he was right on the verge of falling in love with her.

"You should have been in the movies," Anne had told him one day. "The way you can turn on the charm, without even trying to do it. And the way the gals fall for it."

"But you don't fall for it. Do you, Anne? Perhaps if you were to—"

"I work for you," Anne had reminded him with a quick grimace. "I see you at your worst. I know what a slave-driver you are, and what a terrible temper you have, and what a mean, nasty disposition you display when things don't go to suit you."

"Little liar."

Anne had wrinkled her nose at him, her eyes mischievous. Of course she was lying, deliberately teasing him.

It was a temptation to tease him, after watching some woman client gush and purr and make such a silly to-do over him as so many of them did. Someone, she reminded him, had to cut him down to size every so often, or he'd get much too big for his britches. And furthermore, there had to be at least one girl in town who hadn't fallen madly in love with him at one time or another; one girl who didn't look as if she were about to melt into oblivion under his dark-eyed gaze, his winning smile.

"So you've elected yourself to be the gal who is completely immune!"

"Maybe simply the gal who intends to play it safe."

"You cast aside my charm as a mere nothing and bait me—all in the same breath. My girl, I have my suspicions of you. Perhaps you are as indifferent as you pretend. And on the other hand, perhaps you are up to some deep and clever design. To catch me when I'm not looking, so to speak. Anne, I have a great notion to fire you and hire me a middle-aged gal with a sound character, thick ankles, and a spreading hip line. Then I'd know I was really safe."

"Go ahead! Shall I write out my resignation or

submit to the humiliation of being fired outright?"

He would, Anne knew, have doubled her salary rather than let her go, and he was already paying her well. A good basic salary, and in addition, a bonus on every big case that he handled.

Alex had told her more than once that she was the only secretary he had ever had who didn't get on his nerves, who handled his work to suit him. His letters came out the way he had dictated them. There was never any need for him to check up to make sure Anne had typed his briefs correctly. She had learned how to hunt up references, check back to ruling decisions on such and such a legal question. She had such a knack for the work that Alex had complimented her once, suggesting kiddingly, "Anne, you should be a woman lawyer."

But when she had taken him seriously, wondering if it wouldn't be an idea for her to take a law course, he had given her a look of mild horror. "Heaven forbid, Anne."

A woman lawyer, to his mind, was a kind of monstrosity which invariably suggested the picture of some hybrid creature with stringy hair, bulging eyes, and flat feet. True, he had never happened to see a female lawyer who resembled in the least this unpleasant preconceived idea. Furthermore, he had run into one or two graduate women lawyers who looked like perfectly normal human beings. Except for an argumentative streak which he disliked in women, they were fairly attractive.

But not for Anne. "You just stick along with me, kid," he advised her. "Maybe one of these days you'll get sick of office work and make up your mind to marry me." This last, of course, was always said with a grin and was intended, as they both understood, as a joke.

Alex would have fired her immediately, had she ever shown any signs of falling in love with him. At least so Anne thought.

But he had known that he was perfectly safe with her. Long before anyone else, Alex had been the one to guess that Kenny was the one. Once he had even gone so far as to give her advice about how to "land Kenny," only to have Anne give him a quickly reproachful look. "You ought to know me better than that, Alex. If I have to resort to silly little schemes and tricks—if he doesn't come to me of his own accord, I don't want him."

This, Alex informed her instantly, was arrant nonsense. He suggested that Anne wasn't quite as bright as he had thought her. "My pet, if women stopped scheming and using tricks to catch their men, the institution of marriage would fold up and soon be as dead as the dodo."

There was just one appropriate retort, and with a quick laugh, Anne tossed it right at him. "Do tell! And that from you, of all people. You, Alex Brooks. You! And what became of all the schemes and traps to lure you into marriage, if schemes and clever little tricks are what it takes?"

Oh, well, Alex was the exception that proved the rule. That was all there was to that. And even Alex, so he declared, went about with his fingers crossed. Sooner or later he would take the step. "Now if you were to go to work on me, Anne, darn if I know what might happen. Before you know it, I might find myself rigged out in a bit and bridle."

The conversation, just when it threatened to become too serious, would end on that note—gay, nonsensical, meaning nothing at all, except that they were friends as well as working partners. For during the nearly two years that Anne had worked in his office, they had learned how to take each other in stride.

They got along beautifully. Practically the only time there was even a hint of friction was when Alex felt his work crowding him. Then he might become short-tempered, impatient, and call Anne down for some very minor thing.

She had learned to pay no attention to him when he was in such a mood. She knew it was simply that he was tired and overworked, his nerves frayed. "I think you need a vacation," was her way of advising him to calm down and take it easy.

Anne found him in one of these upset states, pacing the floor, chain-smoking furiously, on that September morning when she reached the office over an hour later than usual.

"Well," Alex said cuttingly, "I thought maybe you'd decided to retire and apply for your old-age benefits." There was an excuse for him. The phone had been ringing constantly, interfering with his study of the ten-thousand-dollar damage suit case he was taking into court that afternoon. An important witness, one he had been depending on to win his case, had been rushed to the hospital for an emergency operation. He had an aching tooth, which meant a trip to the dentist—an ordeal which always put him off balance. In addition to all that, he had got up feeling rocky, due to over indulgence in liquor and food at a late party the night before. The cumulative effect made him ready to snap at the first target which presented itself, and that turned out to be Anne.

Anne, who was usually so prompt and alert, roamed in at nearly ten-thirty, acting as though her job were the last and certainly the least important thing on her mind.

Accustomed to her usually mild demeanor, Alex was amazed at her peppery retort. "Do you have to get sarcastic, simply because I'm a little late? It doesn't happen often, and you know it. I'm always giving up my evenings to help you get extra work cleaned up and I don't recall that I ever got cute and sarcastic when you asked me to come back after dinner. If you don't like it because I happen to show up late once, you can begin hunting yourself another secretary. You won't be hurting my feelings."

Alex dragged his swivel chair around and stared at her. "Well! What's got into you this morning? Get out on the wrong side of the bed?"

"No." Anne glared at him. "Maybe my mistake was getting up at all." Then she turned her back on him and marched back to the small adjoining office where she had her own desk, typewriter and files.

She had all of her working paraphernalia out and was already busy, typing like mad, when Alex came strolling into the room. He stood lounging against the door frame, watching her. It was a moment before he spoke. "I'm sorry, Anne. I shouldn't have made that crack when you came in."

She kept right on typing, not looking up. "It's all right, Alex. No hard feelings either way, I hope. I guess I'm a little edgy this morning."

"Me too," said Alex.

He lit another cigarette, continuing to watch her until it was smoked halfway down. Then: "What's wrong, kid? You and Kenny have a quarrel? And don't tell me it's none of my business. That I know perfectly well."

Anne shook her head. "No. I haven't quarreled with Kenny. Everything with Kenny is fine. Just fine."

"Good. Glad to hear it. Always glad to hear that young love is going smoothly and well—as young love should go and practically never does. Incidentally, I don't believe a word of it. You marched in here with a chip on your shoulder and you look like a rubber band getting ready to snap."

He strolled over to her desk and stood looking over her shoulder at the sheet of paper inserted in the typewriter. Then, chuckling: "Messiest piece of typing I've ever seen you do. Three erasures in one line, two in the next. Let up, girl." And his hand was a friendly touch on her shoulder. "That letter can't go out and you know it. Come on. Spill it to papa. What's wrong."

Anne said carefully, through set teeth: "I wish you'd go back to your own office. I wish you'd let me alone. There's nothing wrong, truly. I'm just a little nervous, that's all. A touch of a headache. Please, Alex. You have that big case in court today to worry about. I'll be all right in a little while." Her teeth sank deep into her underlip. She still wouldn't look at him.

"Sure, I know. There's nothing wrong. But whatever it is, you'll soon be all right. You just have a touch of a headache—only you happen to be the gal who never gets headaches. And you can just forget about that court case. I'm going to have to ask for a postponement. My leading witness is in the hospital, and that's that. My desk is cluttered up with work and there isn't a single bit of it that can't wait. I feel edgy this morning and I'll admit it, but it's mainly because I ought to cut out parties where I drink too much and eat too much to help forget how bored I am."

He walked around and straddled the edge of her desk. "Come on, Anne. Spill it. And there's no use pretending there isn't something upsetting on your mind. I know you too well."

She looked up at him then, and he saw the troubled unhappiness in her midnight-blue eyes, saw her mouth working before she managed to say: "It's nothing, really. Only I'm such an idiot. That's all, Alex. Truly. Just that I haven't very much sense. We heard from Eileen this morning. She's breaking up with Bob, coming home. And I— Kenny—"

"And you're afraid that Kenny is still in love with her." Alex let her have it, like a knife thrust straight at the heart of an already quivering wound.

"Yes," Anne said stiffly.

Not another soul would have won that quick, all-embracing admission from her. But Alex was different. Her confidences were safe with Alex, and she could trust him neither to humiliate her with pity nor to try to bolster her up with pretty little flattering lies.

"Well, you're crazy," Alex said finally, "if that's all you can find to worry about."

He added savagely: "If Kenny Wilcox is still fool enough to prefer Eileen to you—and I don't believe for one minute that he does or will—then he isn't worth bothering about."

"But you know how it was with them," Anne said

seriously. "For a while Eileen was wildly in love with Kenny."

"Rubbish. Eileen was never in love with anyone except Eileen."

"Well, Kenny was crazy in love with her. That you can't deny."

"Puppy love," said Alex scornfully.

"Perhaps. But what was puppy love yesterday might still be the love of a grown man today. I guess it's just that I've never been really sure that Kenny ever got over Eileen. Maybe I'm just dreaming up trouble and I hope it turns out that way. Maybe it's just that I've always been jealous of Eileen and that's a thing I'm ashamed to confess. I wouldn't admit it to anyone but you, Alex. I don't want people to know I'm so—so small and despicable. I thought I had gotten over it."

How many times, this last year or so, she had smiled over her childish envy of Eileen, over the many small irritations, half forgotten now, at hearing people say: "Well, I guess poor Anne's nose is out of joint, what with Eileen getting so much attention." A baby crying and raging because the other sister held the limelight. That was what it had all amounted to. And thank heavens she had grown out of it, grown up. Secure in her own right, secure in the love of the man to whom her own heart belonged so utterly.

Only she hadn't been secure at all, and it had been a shock to learn it. She was not really grown up, and she felt no real security in Kenny's love. With nothing more alarming to go on than the rearing heads of her own foolish fears, she seemed to feel disaster swooping down on her.

Alex shook his head sorrowfully. "Too bad. Such a sensible girl in so many ways. Such a little nitwit in others. Know your whole trouble, my pretty pet? You have the world's worst inferiority feelings."

"Who wouldn't have?" said Anne, not denying it. "I'm not beautiful. I possess no irresistible charm for men. When I wear a new dress, no one ever notices it. No matter what I wear, or what I do, or where I go, or whom I meet, I'm just the same old Anne. Such a *nice* girl. Such a *sweet* girl. Such a *sensible* girl." There was venom in the words, and Alex threw back his head and shouted with laughter, which made her furious.

"Go on. Laugh at me. Laugh your head off. I know I'm funny."

"Sure you are, honey, very funny when you explode like that. Any second now I expect to see you spitting fire."

"Well, you wouldn't find it very funny, Alex Brooks, if you were me. It isn't a bit funny to be a mousy female who looks as if she'd been born into this world to spend gay, riotous evenings as a baby sitter or something. And what's more—"

Alex exploded with laughter again. Then, seriously, he asked her: "Do you mean to tell me that you believe all that rot you've been saying?"

Why wouldn't she believe it? Anne demanded. Didn't the record of her whole life prove her point?

Had there ever been a line of men forming to the right at *her* door, begging for dates with her?

Had anybody ever voted *her* Beautiful Miss Anything?

Had men ever tossed their breaking hearts under her heel and told her to go ahead and finish up the job of trampling over them?

"I've heard enough," said Alex firmly.

If she must chatter such absurd nonsense, she should go home and shut herself up in her own room and chatter to herself. "You should consult a psychonanalyst," he advsed her solemnly. "It's too big a job for me to attempt. I don't feel equal to it, although I recognize the need."

He shook his head, his eyes watching her. "Good Lord. For my money, you have far more claim to genuine beauty than Eileen. Although I'll grant you this much—you do nothing to bring it out. But it's there and you needn't laugh. If you won't take my word for it, you might cast your harrassed little mind back to a certain artist, Julian Lowry by name.

"Remember Julian, honey? Well, do you? Remember what happened when Julian came to Hillview for the summer and all the eager mamas were after him to do pictures of their daughters? Remember, Anne?"

Julian Lowry! Anne remembered very well. Briefly, Julian had made people sit up and take notice of her. An artist, still fairly young, but doing work that promised serious recognition one of these days. He had come to Hillview under doctor's orders to let down and take it easy for three or four months.

Unwilling, or perhaps temperamentally incapable of spending week after week doing nothing, he had decided to do one painting during his vacation period. Something to be included in the one man exhibit he was planning to give in New York within the next year. He had proved, however, extremely finicky and choosy about his model. None of the recognized beauties of the town seemed to suit him, but when he had discovered Anne one day, by sheer accident, he had walked over to her, introduced himself, and three days later Anne had found herself sitting as his model in the room he had rented and rigged up as a temporary studio.

She gave Alex a rueful grin. "So Julian wanted to do my portrait. And what does that prove? He talked a lot about the planes of my face, about my being a type. But even he never claimed that I was any beauty." She laughed. "He made me loosen my hair; then he put a yellow scarf around my neck, stuck a red rose in my hand and came up with a picture that didn't look an awful lot like me."

"Maybe it looked more like you than you look like

yourself, Anne," Alex said slowly.

"What a curious thing to say, Alex. And anyway—" Anne frowned, remembering her feeling of vague disappointment when Julian had let her take her first look at the finished canvas. "I never cared a lot for the picture."

"I did," Alex declared. "I thought it was lovely. I liked it so well that I made up my mind to own it some day."

"You're just saying that. It isn't like you, Alex, to feed me pretty lies to bolster up my ego. That, of course, is what you're trying to do."

"Am I?" He studied her thoughtfully, then went abruptly back to his own office. He returned with a letter which he told Anne to read. It was an acknowledgement of a letter from himself, under the letterhead of a famous New York gallery. It said that his check had been received, in payment for the painting by Julian Lowry, Girl In A Yellow Scarf, which had recently won a prize in a showing by this artist. The painting would be transmitted to him in due course.

"You mean," said Anne, unbelieving, "that you've actually bought that picture?"

"I've bought it," Alex said emphatically. "I mean to hang it in my study, where I can look at it often. I mean to keep it always, and as you know, I'm not the kind of a guy who wants a place cluttered up with works of art. That painting is alive, and that's what I like about it. It caught your expression so completely that when I looked at it I felt as if you were smiling straight at me, getting ready to speak."

He said: "In a sense, it's more alive than you yourself are, Anne. It has a vitality which you seem to keep under lock and key. The eyes in it have a warmth and longing which you must feel, but don't want anyone to see or know about." He said: "To me it is very lovely, and so are you, Anne. So are you."

For a moment their eyes met squarely. Then Anne laughed. "Such a conversation," she said lightly. "And right in the middle of a busy morning with both of our desks cluttered with work to be done."

"Hang the work."

Many times, in the past, they had had personal conversations. But never one quite like this. Very carefully, in his relations with girls, even with Anne who had his complete confidence, Alex avoided the intense, too personal note. Yet now Anne didn't know what to make of him. Why should he have wanted to possess that picture of her? A passing whim? Possibly. He was not wealthy, yet neither did he have to consider the dimes and dollars. Once, Anne knew, he had bought a vase of antique ruby glass, because the lovely shade of it had intrigued him. Yet later, disliking the shape, he had donated it to a rummage sale. Would the painting of herself end up at a rummage sale?

Intrigued, faintly amused at that prospect, she suggested it, laughing, and Alex astonished her by asserting angrily: "Sometimes I get completely out of patience with you, Anne. Do you get some neurotic pleasure out of cheapening and minimizing yourself?"

He lit a fresh cigarette, paced scowlingly back and forth across the small room, exhaling smoke in a blue cloud. Then, smearing out the cigarette on a tray, he walked around to her and stood very close, leaning down with his hands on her shoulders. "Look here, Anne, tell me the truth. Are you serious in believing that Kenny may still be in love with Eileen? Or are you simply dreaming up something to worry about?"

"I'm very serious," Anne told him. "And I don't believe I'm simply inventing something to worry about. I haven't any doubts but what Kenny does love me. But is he in love with me, the way he once was with Eileen?" She shook her head. "I just don't know and I have very strong doubts. I can't help remembering how he was about her, and he didn't care who knew it." Her smile was small, wistful. "He's never acted the least bit excited about me. He's fond of me, in a quiet sort of way —we're the best of friends, we have fun together, and I think I could have made him happy, if Eileen weren't coming back into the picture."

She sighed. "But Eileen is coming back."

"And you think, in his heart, Kenny is still in love with her."

Anne managed a jerky laugh. "I wouldn't bet against it." She was silent, then spoke. "I've about decided to return Kenny's ring, tell him all bets are off. I won't put myself through a lot of torture, just wondering what Kenny is thinking. I might just as well break off now and get it over with."

Alex seemed to approve, up to a point. "However," he warned her, "you don't want to put yourself in the light of a meek, self-effacing little thing, who knows your place is in the background when the family beauty is returning. If you're going to break the engagement, honey, do it with gestures and an air. Don't tell Kenny you're stepping out because you think he doesn't want you any more; let him think there's someone else *you* want. Tell him there's another man in your life."

"But there isn't." Then, staring straight into his eyes, she felt amazement or shock quicken her blood. Her face, whitening, went even whiter when she heard him saying: "Tell him you want to be freed from your promise to him because you want to marry me."

Then, his hands tightening on her shoulders, his eyes still raking hers, Alex said in an even tone: "Well, how about it? Isn't that an idea? It will save your pride, and," his grin was very faint, "certainly give the town plenty to talk about."

For a moment, too astonished to speak, Anne simply sat and stared back at him. Then, deciding that Alex was having his little joke, she laughed shakily. "My goodness, you had me scared for a minute. I thought you were serious."

"And what makes you so sure that I'm not serious?"

She said quietly, smiling a little: "Now, Alex, I know perfectly well that you have no idea of marrying anyone. Certainly not me. If you're simply offering to let me play at being engaged to you to save my face and my pride—well, that's thoughtful of you. But a little childish, don't you think? And I don't believe it would work because Kenny wouldn't believe it. No one would."

His eyes were still intent on her face, watchful, but by no means cold. He brushed aside her faint: "Let's be sensible and go back to work." He told her: "If you must have it that I'm simply offering you a face-saving, phony engagement, then have it that way. And frankly, I have no idea of breaking down and making ardent love to a girl who is in love with another man. But as a good friend I sincerely advise you not to let Kenny think you are stepping out of his life simply because you think he no longer wants you. And also as a friend—" His tone changed, holding a note she had never heard there before.

He was pulling her to her feet. He actually had his arms around her, and for a second she glimpsed his eyes and the look in them left her shaken, unbelieving.

Then she felt his lips, hard and eager against her own.

Then: "Don't be too sure that this is simply a phony engagement I'm offering you, or you may be in for the surprise of your life." The implication behind the words was so astonishing that later, after she had left the office, she could not be sure that he had really said them.

CHAPTER 3

At eleven o'clock, Anne found herself on the way back home again. Alex, groaning over the mountain of work facing both of them, had decided—in line with his completely contradictory mood of the morning—to shut up shop and not do any work at all.

He would see about the postponement of that court case; then he meant to get in his car and go up to the mountains for a day or two of trout fishing. Anne could consider herself on vacation for the next three days. And if she was meeting Kenny for lunch, "Go home first," Alex had advised her shortly. "Do something about your looks. I don't know just what, but something. Another shade of lipstick, perhaps. Some costume jewelry if you own any, which you probably don't. A red dress, or a yellow one, or even dead white. Anything but that confounded oyster shade. Anything to liven yourself up a little. You should go in more for colors. Without question, you should wear a bright color when you're planning to jilt your young man."

"In other words," Anne had said, amused rather than

offended, "as of the moment, I look like heck."

"Exactly. As of the moment you are a perfect, walking example of a girl no man would turn around to look at twice."

"Such praise! Such a rhapsody of admiration from the man who has spent the last hour berating me for not appreciating my own charms."

He had corrected her. "From the man who has observed you hiding your charms from the world and thinks you haven't very good sense to do it. Consider the pearl, my girl. Hidden away in its oyster shell, it doesn't look like much, I assure you. But polish it up, set it in a pretty velvet box, set a high price on it—"

Grinning, he had shoved her out of the door. "Go home, Anne. Go home and fix up pretty, before you go to meet the boy friend."

It was not too much of a walk, no more than six or seven blocks from the business district. Once on the very outskirts of the town, the house had gradually been crowded in by a newly developed, suburban district to the east, and by the encroachment of business blocks to the west.

"Before you know it," her mother would lament, "we'll have a gas station on the corner and maybe some tacky little shops right in this very block." Nellie, clinging to the old order, refusing to concede that it was a thing of the past, resented and sniffed at every sign of what others called progress.

The way it would end up, according to Nellie, they would be pushed right out of their home—have to sell the property and move into an apartment, which would have its advantages, the servant problem being what it was these days. Only what would become of all their lovely old antique furniture? When Anne, teasing her mother, had suggested that they themselves turn the house into a shop and sell off their antiques, collect more items and start a business, Nellie had gazed at her with pure horror.

Nellie stated solemnly that she had been born a lady and meant to die a lady. And if the time ever came when she had to turn her home into a shop, and start selling all the lovely, lovely antique pieces which helped her to forget all of the dreadful, horrible things that were happening in the world—*well*. Her shocked expression implied that she would much prefer to curl up and die.

When Anne reached the house that morning, she found Aunt Molly Graham on the front porch, rocking placidly and looking over the morning paper. She was a spare, angular woman, with a sharp tongue, gentle brown eyes, and a large store of common sense which had convinced her, years ago, that it was nonsense to try to keep up a big house just for two people. She had persuaded Ned to turn their place, almost as large as the Veigh house, into a tourists' home, and put a house-keeper in charge. Then she and Ned had moved into a three room apartment in a big, modern building right on the corner of Main and Church Streets.

There was practically no work to do, they had every convenience, and in the evening she and Ned could sit at the front window and see all the bright lights and watch the people going into the Majestic Theatre right across the street. Molly considered it the only way to live. She considered Nellie a fool for trying to keep up this big house.

"Your mother," Molly had once said to Anne, "always did like to play the great lady, even when she was a little girl. She still fancies herself as the lady of the manor, and that's the reason she insists on living on in this old barn. Only trouble is, Nellie hates work and always did. At home, she always managed to sneak out of the dirty, messy jobs, and she hasn't changed. And it's impossible to get servants nowadays, even if she could afford to pay them half decent wages, which she can't. So this old heap hasn't been really clean in twenty years. It's cold and draughty in winter, and sort of clammy in summer because the sun doesn't get to it properly. Why she insists on staying here, especially now that Eileen's married and gone, I'll never know!"

"Oh, well," Anne had laughed, "you know Mother. Maybe she's looking forward to the day when Eileen comes home with one or two babies."

"Hello, there." Momentarily, Aunt Molly stopped rocking when Anne came up on the porch. She laid down her paper, took off her reading glasses and looked at Anne closely. This was Aunt Molly's way. Each time they met, even if it was twice in the same day, the older woman would scrutinize Anne as closely as if she hadn't seen her in years. There was, however, great kindness in her glance. Anne had always been her favorite. To her, Eileen was as spoiled and conceited a girl as Molly Graham ever hoped to see. Mostly her mother's fault, of course.

Having reported that Nellie had driven up town for something or other, Molly said: "Your mother tells me that Eileen is coming home. No surprise to me, I must say. Never expected that marriage to last."

Anne, consulting her wrist watch, decided that she had time to sit down and visit with Aunt Molly for a few minutes. She drew up a low wicker chair. With a short laugh: "Are you like Mother? Never thought Bob was good enough for Eileen?"

"Nonsense. He was too good for her. Always thought he'd discover it some day and put her out." Then, regretfully: "Not that I imagine anything of the sort happened. Eileen is probably tired of married life and wants a change. She never really grew up. That's the trouble. Not the child's fault, of course. Nellie spoiled her, everybody spoiled her, guess she expected the world and that nice young husband to go right on spoiling and pampering and catering to her. When they didn't, he probably up and walked out."

Always able to talk more freely to her aunt than to her own mother, Anne said smilingly: "You seem to agree with me, Aunt Molly. I said something of that sort to Mother and she got perfectly furious with me. Perhaps I shouldn't have said it."

Aunt Molly gave her another of those shrewd, penetrating glances before she said testily: "Anne, if you let that sister of yours push you into the background when she comes back, I'll want to give you the spanking of your life. And if she starts any funny business with Kenny Wilcox—"

Anne said quietly: "She'll be perfectly free to start anything she likes with Kenny. If she wants him back, if he still wants her—well, they won't find me standing in the way. And what's more," Anne's head went back, proud, determined, "I don't mean to wait around to find out if Kenny wants to jilt me. I think it will be much more pleasant to be the one who does the jilting. Don't you agree with me, Aunt Molly?"

Their eyes met—the eyes of age and the eyes of youth, yet strangely alike for a moment because of a fierce pride and integrity of spirit which shone in them. And Anne knew perfectly well that Aunt Molly was remembering and thinking: History repeating itself.

Aunt Molly, Anne knew, might have been her own mother, for she had loved Tom Veigh first. He, according to family rumors, had been deeply in love with her. But a week before their engagement was to have been announced at a big dance in the hotel ballroom young Nellie, pretty as a picture and all gay and sparkling and very sure of herself after a year's travel in Europe, had arrived home. "I have a great notion to steal Tom Veigh away from you," Nellie had informed her sister, laughing of course, the very first night she met him.

Three months later, Tom had married Nellie. Or—according to those who believed that Nellie had played a mean, cruel, unforgivable trick on her older and less artful sister—Nellie had married Tom.

For a moment, the remembering was all there in the older woman's eyes. The grief she had once known, the agonized tears she had shed, the passion at the core of her being, like a bright torch refusing to go out, which ripped and tore at her and refused to accept the meaningless emptiness of life without Tom, the unadulterated torture of watching his love given and lavished on the pretty sister whom she'd never liked too well anyway. I can't go on living, her heart had cried. And if she had to she would love Tom Veigh to the day she died.

Well, it had all been a long time ago and remembering her heartbreak was like recalling a far away dream. The pattern was clear enough, but completely without substance. She hadn't loved Tom Veigh for always or even for a full six months after Nellie had stolen him away from her. Because by that time she had met Ned Graham, and within the year they were married. She considered him as good a husband as a woman could ask for, and certainly better than most. She was good friends with Nellie, and held absolutely nothing against her, except the favoritism she had always shown for Eileen over Anne. That positively made Molly boil.

As for the love she had once felt for Tom Veigh— there was nothing more substantial left of it than a bitter-sweet memory, and the faint sadness in her sigh as she looked at Anne and shook her head. "Who am I to tell you what's best to do, child? Kenny is a fine young man, and you're the one I'd like to see get him. You'd make a wonderful doctor's wife, and," the sharpness came back into her tone, "Eileen would probably drive him stark crazy in about six months. Kenny would have an important operation on, and Eileen would pout because he couldn't stay home and admire her new hair-do. But if he still hankers after her—"

Aunt Molly shook her head. After all, what could she say? What dare she say? She didn't believe in telling people what to do, playing God with an airy gesture, because suppose it turned out you were wrong? Then what? Then, unfortunately, you didn't have God's omnipotence about setting things right again.

There was just one thing she wished she knew how to say to Anne, to make her see all clear and true. That no matter how deep the pain of love might go when you were young, it was never as important as you thought and sure to be over long before you believed possible.

If she could only make the girl understand that the

day would come when she would wish with all of her heart that she could know, once again, the pain of love. Because the pain and the heartbreak were all part of the richness and vitality of youth, and only the young could know it truly. She wished that she could cry to her: "Anne, darling, hang onto the pain—if pain you must feel—because even in that there is sweetness. Some day you will know it. Some day, when you are too old to feel much of anything, when your chief worries will be the high price of eggs and the aches in your old bones when you get up in the morning."

It was no use. There was no way at all for age to reach across the chasm of experience and make the young understand the things which they, too, must learn through years of living. So Aunt Molly merely said, very gently: "You are a dear girl, Anne, and I love you with all my heart. Sometimes I wish you had been my own daughter, and no matter what happens, I hope it turns out for the best."

Upstairs, Anne showered quickly. Then, going to her closet to select a fresh frock, she remembered what Alex had said: "Wear a bright color," and it struck her, with a small shock, that she owned no bright-colored dresses. Everything seemed to be an off shade of some more decisive shade, even that oyster dress which Alex had disposed of so thoroughly this morning.

Something not quite so conspicuous, she would say when she went to buy a dress. Was this because she believed that the pale, soft tones were more becoming to her? Or because she instinctively avoided anything daring? Avoided both colors and styles that might possibly attract attention to herself?

Scared little rabbit, she thought, for a moment thoroughly disgusted with herself, with her way of doing everything, with her complete inability to run to meet life gaily, laughingly, throwing a challenge to it as other girls did. As Eileen had always done.

That's all you are. Just a scared little rabbit.

She selected a black and white checked gingham which had a tiny matching jacket. As she slipped the dress over her head, she caught a glimpse of herself in the long door mirror. White limbs, slender delicately curved body, as pretty a figure, really, as a girl could ask for. A lovely, slender statue of a girl.

She walked over to the dressing table and regarded her face in the wide oval mirror which hung above it. Alex had said: "Julian Lowry's painting looked more like you than you look like yourself." Meaning what? And what had Julian, the artist, meant when he had said: "The plane structure of your face is excellent. Really excellent."

She touched the tips of her fingers to high squarish cheekbones, matched by a stubborn little chin with a cleft place in it. Her nose was small and straight, the mouth, with its sweet curve, wide. But when all was said and done, it was just another face, wasn't it? And certainly not one to set the world afire. What was it that she should do? More makeup? But she loathed heavy, garish makeup, and anyway, that sort of thing savored too strongly of those foolish columns of advice to the lovelorn. "Try another shade of lipstick, a touch of eye-shadow, a new hair-do, and first thing you know your skittish young man will be swooning at your feet!"

Rubbish.

Talk was cheap. Artists had been known to prefer downright homely faces, professing to find an elusive beauty in them. And Alex often said things just to be different from other people. He was like that.

Glancing at her wrist watch, Anne realized with a start that she was due to meet Kenny in five minutes. His time was so valuable, she tried never to keep him waiting. She grabbed up her bag and a fresh handker-chief, ran down the stairs. Fortunately, Nellie drove up just as Anne got to the front porch. She could take the car back uptown.

Gordon's Grill, on the opposite corner from the town's largest bank, was right in the heart of the business section. Not a chance of finding a parking place in front of it, Anne knew. She drove the car up a side street and left it there. Then, walking the rest of the way, she had to pass Martha Rizik's dress shop, which reminded Anne that she was due there for a fitting this afternoon. That new evening dress, which she had been deliberately pushing to the back of her mind. The dress she planned to wear at her engagement party!

You're still engaged to Kenny, she reminded herself, so why not stop crossing bridges until you come to them? Stop being so sure that the ground has fallen away from under you. Get a grip on yourself. You might at least wait until you see Kenny, hear what he has to say, before you start being so darned sure that everything is lost. Keep your chin up and use a little bit of sense. Wait. *Wait*.

Lovely, lovely advice. Such sensible advice. Everyone gave her such sound, sensible advice. Alex, Aunt Molly, even herself. But what good did it do? What did it count for? She had that sick, aching lurch in her heart, a lump in her throat, the knowledge deep inside her which was feeling rather than knowing as she told herself sorrowfully: "Your heart knows, has always known, that Kenny's love for you is only second best."

CHAPTER 4

Kenny was late. Fidgety, nervous as a witch, Anne waited in the tiny entrance lobby leading to the dining room. She knew practically everyone in town, and nodded and smiled at several women coming in or going out. A Mrs. Edith Keeler, garrulous and gushing, stopped a moment to talk. "Anne, dear, how is your mother? Tell her I've been meaning to come over to see her, but I'm so busy, busy, busy. And what do you hear from that beautiful sister of yours? And that attractive young man of yours, such a dear boy, such a charming bedside manner, too. My dear, you'll have to watch him closely once you're married. It's such a strain, I should think, having an attractive doctor for a husband. Women have *such* a way of falling in love with their doctors. I've never understood why, but it just seems to happen—" With a coy smile, "When is the wedding to be, Anne? Haven't you set the date yet? Mustn't put it off too long, dear. He's so attractive and attractive men are at such a premium!"

Running down, from sheer exhaustion of breath, the

woman seemed to expect some sort of answer. Anne said, her smile cool, neither friendly nor unfriendly: "Kenny and I are very good friends, Mrs. Keeler. But—"

"Now, now. Don't try to pretend to me, dear. Everyone in town knows how it is between you two. Why, the dear boy never looks at another girl and hasn't for a year and more. I, for one, was so happy about it when he started going with you seriously. He seemed such a long time getting over Eileen. I just wondered if he would ever look at another girl. He seemed to take her marriage so hard, didn't he? Ah, well, better to have loved and lost than never to have loved at all! So nice to have seen you, dear. And tell your mother—"

Darn the woman. Tight with fury, Anne watched her go sailing out with her bundles, her silly platform shoes, her consuming interest in other people's affairs. Anne thought, There goes the whole curious, gossipy, prying town, all wrapped up in Edith Keeler's lumpy figure and babbling tongue. What Edith said, the whole town said. The town was already wondering when her engagement was to be announced, when the marriage was to take place.

The town had never forgotten, would never forget, that Eileen had jilted Kenny. How hard he had taken it.

No doubt now they said between themselves: "He's taking Anne because he couldn't get Eileen."

The whisperings there would be when Eileen came home—the rumors, the wondering. Anne thought:

What a field day they would have if Kenny and I were to break up! She didn't know if she could take it. She thought wildly: "Maybe I'll get out of town.

Her mind was so taken up with that momentary picture of escape that she did not see Kenny come in. She jumped, feeling his hand on her arm. Then his low, attractive voice: "Hello, Anne. Sorry to have kept you waiting."

She had to look up to meet his smiling gray eyes, for she was a small girl and he was a very tall young man.

Tall, attractively lean, with light brown hair, good features, a nice smile that lit up a face otherwise a little on the grave and serious side. Kenny Wilcox had never been a handsome boy and he was not a handsome man. But he had a warmth of personality, coupled with a touch of shyness, which endeared him to people immediately. Some woman in town had once said: "There's something about Kenny that makes every woman and girl he meets want to mother him." Yet, contradictorily, there were few young men who had less need of mothering. He had always been mature beyond his years. Even as a boy, he had been thoughtful, serious-minded, with a real sense of responsibility and a deep intensity of purpose. Which, perhaps, was the reason that Eileen's treatment of him had hit him such a hard blow.

They went into the dining room and found a table by the wall.

They smiled at each other, and Kenny said in that

low voice that always touched her heart like a lovingly pressed hand: "Hello, honey." Anne said, no thanks. No cocktail for her. Sherry? Well, perhaps. She ordered a chicken salad sandwich, coffee. No dessert. She wasn't very hungry. She thought, I've been dreaming up worries all for nothing.

Nothing was changed. Kenny's smile had the same warmth that it always had. His eyes, watching her, held the same deep affection. His voice was the same as ever, seeming to reach across the table to her in love, no matter what the words he was saying. And so did his hand, finding hers, pressing it gently. What had she been worrying about?

Crazy me, she thought. And heard her own laughter, gay, joyous, carefree over nothing at all. For neither of them had said anything very funny. But she laughed with exultance and wonder from the sheer relief of feeling her foolish fears melt away under his reassuring glance.

"Isn't this salad perfectly wonderful?" she said. And the coffee was wonderful. And the pretty, flickering candles on the small tables with their gay yellow cloths. And the rose which their waitress wore tucked in her dark hair, and the laughter of other people, and the talk, and the soft, melodious strains of a Strauss Waltz coming from the radio set in the wall near the ceiling. Oh, everything was wonderful, wonderful, wonderful. Everything in the whole wide world seemed perfect—

colors brighter; the strain of a haunting melody more beguiling; the beat of her own tender heart swifter and free again, because Kenny seemed just the same. And her fears and her worries had been just so much nonsense.

Kenny waited until they had finished the luncheon, were having a second cup of coffee, before he said: "Well, as I told you over the phone, I had a letter from Eileen. I suppose you've heard from her too?"

Anne nodded. "Yes. Mother had a letter. This morning. She's leaving Bob, coming home. I suppose she told you." She looked straight into his eyes. "Does it make any difference to you, Kenny?"

Was it her imagination that his eyes deliberately avoided hers? His answer came quickly enough, accompanied by a faint smile. "Of course not. Why should it?"

Anne told him honestly: "I've been wondering about it all morning. You loved her once. She's coming back, and she may not be another man's wife for long. If I thought that you had any doubts at all—"

She had never seen him show such quick signs of impatience, sharp irritation. He said, frowning: "Listen, Anne, I'm not a callow schoolboy. I don't go about mooning over a girl who tossed me overboard for another man. That's all over and done with and has been for a long time. You and I are engaged, aren't we?"

And as she hesitated, he repeated the question sharply: "Well, aren't we?"

"Yes, of course, Kenny."

"Our engagement is about to be formally announced, isn't it?"

"Yes."

"And I've told you that you're the girl I want for my wife. Haven't I told you that?"

It was his manner, not the words themselves, that quickened her gnawing fears back to life again. His voice, even his look, had never been less lover-like.

He might have been a lawyer putting questions to an unfriendly witness.

He might have been a man trying to convince himself.

He was saying: "What did you think, that I'd start trying to slide out of our engagement because I heard that Eileen was coming back? Is that all you think my love for you amounts to?"

Anne said quietly: "Putting it that way isn't fair to either of us, Kenny. I don't think you'd try to slide out of anything, once you'd given your word. Quite the contrary. You'd probably go through with a bargain you'd made even if it killed you, or meant spoiling your life to do it. It's how you feel, Kenny. That's all I want to know. How do you feel about Eileen's coming home, at the thought of seeing her again, at knowing that she may be back in circulation?"

His quick show of anger was surprising and certainly unreasonable as he bit out the words: "I don't feel anything at all. Does that satisfy you?"

"Yes. Of course." She finished her coffee, gave him a bright smile as she put down her cup. Her hand crept across the small table, touched his gently. "Please don't be cross with me, Kenny. I'm only trying to play completely fair with you. I'm only trying to let you know that I wouldn't try to hold you, if you didn't want to be held. After all," her smile trembled on not too steady lips, "you can't expect me to altogether forget that you sort of fell in love with me on the rebound."

"I did nothing of the sort," he contradicted her instantly. "It's been nearly five years since your sister threw me over and married another guy. It's been, roughly, five weeks since the night I asked you to marry me. I would remind you that much history has been made in that time—that one war has ended, another one started, that you've grown up from a somewhat gawky kid into a mature and very attractive gal during those years. You've grown into the girl I've *told* you I want to marry. And if that's love on the rebound—"

"Skip it," she said quickly. Then, laughing jerkily: "This seems to be my day for a lot of scrambled ideas, for saying all the wrong things." And why try to explain that it was all because she was such a badly frightened girl? A girl sick with fear, shaken with insecurity at the thought of losing the man who, for her, represented all of the things that gave meaning to life, or even made it worth the living.

Instead she reminded him: "When you phoned you

said there was something you wanted to talk over with me. It seemed to be tied up with Eileen's letter. Was it anything important?"

"Very."

He was smiling again, his annoyance apparently forgotten. He stood up and went around the table to pull back her chair for her. He picked up the check, and took her arm. "I have something to show you. I think I've found exactly the apartment for us. If you agree, I'll give you something else to think about. But I warn you, it will call for some very fast thinking."

His tone lent a mystery to the words which puzzled her, and when they reached the pavement outside Anne demanded immediately: "You know how I hate to be kept in suspense, Kenny." Laughing a trifle: "Must I remind you that I'm the gal who never could wait until Christmas morning to open her gifts? All those little tags, 'Don't open until Xmas,' simply don't faze me. I rip right through them." She caught his arm. "Tell me, Kenny. Why am I going to have to do some fast thinking?"

Grinning down at her, he chuckled. "What a kid you are," he said, his voice loving her. "I wonder if I'll ever get used to the idea of having you for my wife? Half the time I'll be imagining you're my kid sister, just as I always have. Well, here's the big idea, honey. How would you like to just run away and get married without telling anybody beforehand?"

Her heart thumped and her eyes grew wide. "You mean elope?"

He laughed. "If you prefer the word with the sentimental story-book touch, yes. That's what I mean. Elope. How about it?"

"But, Kenny, our engagement hasn't even been announced yet."

"Must it be?"

"No. I suppose not." She laughed, but her laughter had a wistful note. After all, she'd been looking forward to her engagement party. She'd been looking forward to all of the gay, happy, completely unimportant preliminaries to marriage to which their very significance lends a very real importance.

The exciting period during which a girl goes tiptoeing toward marriage to her love and the fulfillment of her every dream. The round of parties and dances and showers. Attention focused on herself who, for these few little weeks, for this one and only time in her life, holds the center of the stage. The "getting ready." The selection of the bridal gown. The loving envy of her friends. "Darlng, aren't you simply frantic with excitement? I know I'd be. Think of having that sweet, darling Kenny Wilcox for a husband."

The last days of her girlhood.

The last days before she closes the pages of a fairy tale, and picks up the more solemn book of life which waits for all women, has always waited—marriage.

Oh, it was make-believe, all of it. All of these last little plans and preparations. Not at all important. And why should she be reluctant to give them up? It would be just as beautiful to go off with Kenny and marry him, without any fuss and bother at all. And hadn't she always said that she didn't care a thing about big weddings? Hadn't she said time and time again that she'd just as soon put that extra money in something nice for her future home and just go off and be married quietly by a justice of the peace?

Of course she had said that.

Then why, why, when Kenny suggested doing that very thing, did she feel this sudden constriction of her heart? Why, without any warning at all, did she feel half sick with disappointment?

The answer was to be found in another question. Why, suddenly, was Kenny in such a hurry to get it all over with?

Why, out of a blue sky, did he suggest getting married immediately, before Eileen came home?

The sky was as blue as ever, the sun shone as brightly, and it was as magnificent an early autumn day as could be imagined. But all of the wonder had gone out of the day for Anne.

She said, without much expresson in her voice, "Well, it's something to think about, Kenny."

"Yes, I think so," Kenny said emphatically. "I'm very much in favor of it. Since we're going to be married, and now that I've found this apartment, I see no reason for waiting. It seems sort of silly."

"Yes. I see what you mean, Kenny."

They turned a corner and walked quietly along until they came to where Kenny always left his car parked. Neither of them said a word for several minutes. There didn't seem to be anything to say.

CHAPTER 5

The street to which Kenny drove was, like Anne's own home, in one of the older sections but on the opposite side of town. Here, too, there were a number of large, old-fashioned homes with wide, sweeping lawns in front of them, gardens to the side and back. A double line of towering old maple trees, their leaves already beginning to turn, formed a kind of archway. It was a lovely street. Very lovely.

Kenny drew up and stopped before one of the largest houses, colonial style, with white columns supporting a two story high roof over the wide porch. In its day, this had been the home of one of the town's wealthiest families, among its original founders. But that was now ancient history. The sons and daughters had married and left town. The house, after changing hands several times, had now been remodeled and turned into small apartments. Only the outside retained even a semblance of its former appearance. Inside everything was very modern and up to date.

In Hillview, far more than in many other southern

towns, the housing problem had remained a problem. There was a boys' college nearby, and what with accommodations for the ever increasing number of students and their families, any slack in living quarters was taken up before it had a chance to develop.

In addition, Fort Prendle, used as a marine base during the last war, was now reopening again, which meant still more demand for houses and apartments. Anne and Kenny had talked it over, wondering what their chances, if any, were of finding a suitable place to start their married life in.

It had been a worry. Her own home, of course, was big enough to accommodate three or four families. But move in with her mother? Never! That wasn't Anne's idea of getting married, certainly not to start with. And Kenny had been in perfect agreement with her. He himself, now that his family were gone, had been living in two makeshift, housekeeping rooms over a shop. It was okay for a man who was home very little, except to sleep. An elderly woman, a distant relative, had been living with him, attending to the cleaning, cooking, taking his phone calls for him. It was no place to take a bride.

This angle, which had worried Kenny even more than it had Anne, explained his genuine enthusiasm over this new apartment, which he had heard about only the evening before by the merest accident.

And enthusiastic he was. This was no pretense, Anne

knew, as he led her up three flights of stairs to the top floor and into a not too small apartment which he proceeded to display with pride and something close to excitement.

He made her admire the picture window in the living room, facing down over the garden which, in the spring, would be gay and fragrant with roses. Two bedrooms, one of them very small, of course, but still large enough to hold his medical books and journals and be fitted up as a kind of study.

The kitchen was shining white. It was neither too large nor too small, and it was completely modern, even up to a garbage disposal, something Anne had read about but never actually seen before.

Every room got plenty of sun.

Kenny didn't see how they could possibly do any better, until, of course, the time came for them either to buy or build a place of their own. Which was the thing he was looking forward to, but which was out of the question, as of right now. There was no place in town for sale that he would have, even at half the price. And building couldn't be considered until prices came down a little. "What do you think of it, honey?" he asked finally.

Anne hadn't said very much.

She had walked from one room to another, looked out of windows at the view when he told her to look, admired the features she was expected to admire, agreed, as was expected of her, that everything was very nice. "Yes, Kenny. If we can't have a bath and shower both, I prefer a shower. I really do. And that stall shower is very cute. I like it. I quite agree with you. There's really nothing more important than getting lots of sun in rooms you're living in all the time. Our house never gets enough sun. Some of the rooms stay damp, half the time." She paused.

"Oh, no, Kenny. I wouldn't want a bit more room than there is here. It would just be a lot of useless space to keep clean. Yes, Kenny. No, Kenny. Yes, no, yes, no, yes."

"What the devil's the matter?" he demanded finally. "Don't you like it?"

She stared at him for a moment, fighting back words she wanted with all of her heart not to say. Because once they were spoken—once the harsh, ugly truth was forced out into the open between them— She said carefully: "It's very nice, Kenny. Of course I like it. Why do you think that I don't?"

"Well, you show about as much enthusiasm as if I were inviting you to live in a hospital ward. It's lovely and clean, Kenny. It has lots of nice sun, Kenny. And the sun is so good for you. What's got into you, anyway? Maybe this place isn't good enough for you. Maybe you were expecting to start right out in one of those new places they're asking thirty thousand bucks for. Well, I haven't got that kind of money, and you know it. I don't know when I will have, if ever. And if this isn't good enough for you—"

Anne backed against a wall and for a minute just stood there looking at him. She tried to speak, but before she could get the words to come, the tears came. They streaked down her cheeks and she didn't even try to wipe them away. At first all she could say was, "Oh, Kenny, Kenny, darling." Then:

"I think it's the most beautiful apartment I ever saw! I'd rather live here, with you, than any other place in the whole wide world. I could be happy here, for always, if only—"

Her trembling hands reached out to him in a piteous gesture, then dropped to her sides. She kept shaking her head slowly. "You said it all a little while ago, darling, without knowing what you said: 'Half the time I'll be imagining you're my kid sister, just as I always have.' That's the way you love me, Kenny. Like a sister. Your heart knows it while your mind keeps trying to deny it."

She took a long, sighing breath. "You're afraid, Kenny. You're terribly afraid. That's why you want to get married immediately and get settled in this apartment before Eileen gets back. You're afraid of what will happen when you see her again. You're afraid of yourself. You think if we were already married, if it was an established fact and no going back, it would be a protection. You think it would be insurance against hurting me, against going back on your promise to me."

She managed a small, tight smile. "It wouldn't work, darling. Believe me, it just wouldn't work. If Eileen still has a hold on your heart, being married to a girl you love like a sister wouldn't break it. You'd be miserable. And in the end so would I." She repeated it slowly: "And so would I."

He had not spoken. When Anne walked slowly over to him, his hands reached for her, he held her a little away from him, studying her, but still he did not speak. She looked straight into his eyes and she saw the troubled uncertainty, the pain in them. They were warm with tenderness, and the thought of his tenderness moved her deeply, brought the quick tears back to her eyes.

She thought, He'd rather be hurt himself than hurt me. She was tempted, momentarily, to offer him the easy way out. Alex's way! If she were to say to him: "Alex Brooks has asked me to marry him," it would save her own pride, and Kenny's too. But to be less than honest with Kenny? To resort to schoolgirlish pretense, a pretty, face-saving lie? She knew that she couldn't do it. There must always be truth between her and Kenny. Anything less was simply not good enough.

Impulsively she put her hands to his cheeks, and now it was not too hard to smile. "Look, Kenny, let's be grown up about it, and completely honest with each other. Once upon a time you were wildly in love with my sister. It hit you a terrific wallop when she married someone else. In time, you managed to bury your feelings so deep that you believed they were dead. But when you learned she was coming home, and maybe without a husband, the protective covering slit right down the middle. You started remembering a thousand things you thought were forgotten forever, and right this minute you don't actually know for sure whether you're still in love with Eileen or not. Isn't that the truth of it, Kenny? Isn't it?"

When he still didn't answer, she said a little angrily: "I don't want to be treated like a child, Kenny. I'm not a frail little blossom that's going to wilt on the vine if I have to give you up. I won't enjoy it but I can take it. What I can't and won't take is to be lied to because you feel sorry for me. And I won't be married out of pity, either," she cried with considerable spirit. "That's the worst insult you could possibly offer me. To try to rush me into an immediate marriage because you were afraid if you waited a few weeks you just couldn't go through with it! Now I want the truth, Kenny."

She caught his arms and gave them a vigorous shake. "Do you understand, Kenny Wilcox? I want the truth."

He spoke then, very quietly. "Will you believe me, Anne, if I tell you that I don't know what the truth is? I just don't know."

Kenny brushed one hand over his eyes in a weary gesture, then walked over to the window and stood staring down into the garden where the roses that had bloomed so gorgeously a few weeks ago were already dying. He spoke very low. "I thought that I was completely over it, a long time ago. I haven't given Eileen more than a passing thought in weeks, months. I'd have sworn that she no longer meant a thing to me. But when her letter came this morning—"

Again he passed his hand over his eyes, and it might have been the gesture of a man who could not see very clearly. He shook his head slowly. "I can't tell you what the truth is, Anne, because I just don't know. I feel unsure about everything. I thought if we got married immediately, it would be something firm and certain to hold to, and that then my doubts would go away."

He turned to her, and his gray eyes were dark and shining with a deep and abiding tenderness. He took her gently into his arms. "This much I can tell you for sure, Anne. You are sweet and fine and true, and everything that I want in a wife. Everything. You are good. I know that there isn't a mean or a disloyal streak in you. I would trust my life, my future with you. I would trust my hopes and my plans with you and know that you would never fail me. I know that when you marry, it will be for worse as well as for better, and that if the going got tough, you'd be right in there pitching beside me. I know that you're the kind of a girl who would stick, always. And I have wanted you for my girl. With all of my heart I have wanted that, sweetheart. I still do."

His tone harshened, and his arms tightened convulsively around her as he repeated, "I still want you for my girl! And yet—"

He let her go, and one hand fumbled in his pocket for a cigarette. "Having said all that, you'll probably call me a liar when I tell you, honestly, that I still don't know what I feel about Eileen. Or will feel."

He turned back to the window, his softly murmured words might have been spoken to himself. "It was a kind of madness, what I felt for her, and I do not know if the madness is over." He shook his head slowly. "I just don't know."

It was easier to do than Anne would have thought possible. And perhaps that was because all she could feel for the moment was a kind of helpless numbness. The capacity to feel pain or hurt or even shock seemed to have gone out of her.

She walked across the room and got her bag from the radiator where she had left it when they came in. She opened it and took out the ring with the small diamond in it. She had been waiting to wear it in public until their engagement had been formally announced. She walked back to Kenny, who was still standing staring dismally out of the window.

When Anne put the ring in his hand, he stared at it for a moment, shifting it about in his palm. Then, with a short laugh: "Well, it wasn't much of a ring anyway, was it?" And he slipped it carelessly into his pocket.

Anne stood close beside him, yet was careful not to

touch him as she said slowly, her voice under perfect control: "Let's not be dramatic about it, Kenny. Let's just say we both want a little more time to make up our minds. And I hope we can go right on being the same good friends we've always been."

"Oh, skip it," Kenny said savagely. "For Pete's sake, skip all the corny lines about remaining good friends and all the rest of it. That I can't take."

"*You* can't take it." Anne stared at him with quietly angry eyes. "I thought I was the one who was having to take plenty."

"That's just it. No matter how you pretty it up with sensible talk, you're the one who's taking the dirty end of the stick, and it makes me feel like a first-class heel."

CHAPTER 6

When Anne went home, late that afternoon, her mother was fluttering and darting about like an excited butterfly. Another letter had come, special delivery, from Eileen. In the first letter she had been vague about the date of her return. Possibly ten days, she had written. Now, a few hours later, she was coming in three days.

Anne thought, knowing Eileen, she'll be here when she gets here. And that would be when she thought she had stirred up sufficient excitement and suspense about her arrival.

Once Uncle Ned had said, laughing: "Our Eileen is the type who isn't satisfied unless she's the bride at the wedding and the corpse at the funeral." And it was true. Never, even when she was a child, had Eileen been happy unless all attention was focused upon herself. Her entrances into rooms had to be made with a dramatic flourish, her easily wept tears more bitter and racking than any average tears. She had all of the qualifications for a star of the silver screen, except any real ability to act. Now, Anne knew, her homecoming would have to be done with gestures.

Anne sighed to herself. It was wearying even to think about. Still more wearying to hear her mother saying worriedly: "There's so much to be done before she gets here. We must get all the silver polished and Eileen's old room must be opened up and aired and cleaned. I'd like to put up new drapes and curtains, but there just isn't time. So we'll just have to take down the old ones and wash and iron them, and what about that new chair you bought for your bedroom, Anne? Don't you think it would be nice to put it in Eileen's room?"

"No, I don't think so," Anne said, and was a little ashamed of her curt tone. But she had bought that chair with her own money, for the express purpose of having a comfortable place to sit and read late at night. As she often did. And why should she be expected to hand it over to Eileen, who had probably never read a book through in her whole life, and who used a bedroom for nothing except to sleep in and to dress and preen herself and admire herself before the mirrors?

"Don't you think you're being a little selfish?" Nellie asked, gently reproachful.

Anne smiled. Selfish. It was a word she was accustomed to, where Eileen was concerned. In the old days, her mother had invariably accused her of selfishness if she protested against giving in to Eileen's slightest whim.

Nellie wasn't to be blamed. If anything, she was to be pitied. It was that complete blind spot she had where Eileen was concerned. Oddly, Anne had never felt any deep hurt because Eileen was their mother's favorite. But she had always resented being expected to give up the best of everything to her sister. Now that she was older, earning her own money, she was prepared to stand up for her own rights, so far as the little things were concerned.

She would not give up her pretty, chintz-covered easy chair. Nor the hooked rug, lovely with its soft pastel shades, beside her bed.

I may have to give up Kenny to her, Anne thought drearily. I may have to hand her over my love, the only thing in life that really matters! But I won't give her my chair or my rug. I won't let her have the things that don't matter in the least.

"I've given Kenny back his ring," Anne announced, over dinner that evening. Might as well get it said and over with. Her mother would have to know before long, anyway. So say the words. Get used to the horrible, ugly sound of them.

Get used to that iron band constricting her heart.

Get used to the feel of not having him any more. Get used to the emptiness, the loneliness, the intolerable pointlessness of everything that she did. The steps that she took, the words that she spoke. Embrace the pain! Get used to it, once and for all, because she was going to have to live with it for a long, long time. Perhaps forever. Or so it seemed to her now.

Nellie was busy with a carving knife, cutting slices off of a leg of lamb, when Anne broke the news. "Really?" she said, pausing for no more than a second or two, then going right on with the business of carving. "Some peas, Anne? These are lovely and fresh. And I want to know how you like that pear salad. It's a new recipe. I thought I'd try it and see how we like it; then we can have it when Eileen comes. She's so fond of dainty, unusual dishes."

Anne could have screamed.

She wanted to cry: "Doesn't it make any difference to you that I'm unhappy? Is a pear salad for Eileen more important to you than my breaking heart?" Almost immediately her sense of humor got the best of her. After all, hearts didn't actually break. Certainly not hers. And she would have been the first to resent any show of maudlin pity. So perhaps Nellie was taking it in the very best way.

Presently her mother came back to the subject. "Well, I think you've done a very sensible thing, Anne. I suppose it was because of Eileen and I hardly see how you could have done otherwise. I know that Kenny is very fond of you and he would be a good husband. But I've never believed a girl can find much happiness with a man who's hopelessly in love with another woman. And Kenny was so absolutely *wild* about Eileen. I've never believed that he really got over it. I've never thought that he loved you in the same way that he did her."

It was the smug complacency of Nellie's tone that Anne resented. And, still more resentful, she heard her saying brightly: "Of course, I haven't any idea whether or not Eileen would want Kenny back again. Likely as not, she wouldn't even look at him. Still, I can understand how the dear boy feels. Naturally, he's hopeful. And if Eileen were to show any interest in him, I wouldn't have a word to say against it. She could certainly do worse. *Did* do worse, when she took up with Bob Thompson."

Anne stared at her mother briefly. Then, knowing her nerves were near the breaking point, she pushed back her chair. "I'm young and healthy, and supposed to have lots of good rich blood. Would you like me to have myself bled, so I can turn several quarts of that over to Eileen, too, Mother?"

Nellie, looking perfectly solemn, was slow in grasping the sarcasm. When she did, she looked hurt. "Now, Anne, you mustn't take things I say in that spirit. You must remember that Eileen has had a very hard time of it. Her marriage has gone wrong. When she comes home, she will have to make a complete new adjustment to life. If I seem overly anxious about her—"

"Well, my engagement has gone wrong and I may have to make a few new adjustments myself."

"Oh, Anne, for heaven's sake. Come back here and sit down and finish your dinner. I have some nice tapioca pudding for dessert. Anne, dear, please. I'll be very much hurt if you persist in acting this way."

But Anne was already on her way out of the room. "I'm sorry, Mother. I'm not hungry. I really couldn't eat another bite."

Nor could she hang around this house for the rest of the long, lonely, empty evening. The first, she supposed, of endless more lonely, empty evenings—an eternity of such evenings—when Kenny would not be coming, or phoning to arrange to meet her at the corner in front of the Hillview Hotel or to say that he was being held up by an emergency call and would be delayed for half an hour or so.

He won't be coming any more. Kenny won't be coming any more—it's all over, all over, all over. The words, pitiless, holding her doom from which there was no escape, were like drops of burning acid spilling slowly over her heart. For by now the pain and the awareness of what it all meant had started in for fair.

She was going down the first of those long, steep, difficult steps into the complete consciousness that her love was lost forever. She had never known before what the pain and hurt of love could really mean. But now she knew. Or was beginning to find out.

Anne went upstairs, bathed her face and changed her dress, then, coming downstairs again, called back to her mother in the kitchen to say that she was going out for a walk. She might go to the movies. When Nellie called back, "If you wait a few minutes, Anne, I'll run upstairs and dress and we could go to the movies together," Anne knew that it was her mother's way of trying to make amends.

Well, that was okay. Anne wasn't holding any grudge, nor indulging in self-pity. But her every need, right now, was to get off by herself. She called back, perfectly friendly: "If you don't mind, Mother, I think I'd rather go alone."

Yet when she got outside and was on her way uptown, her loneliness seemed almost more than she could bear.

She thought, reverting to an infantile longing for love and to be made to feel secure, If only I had someone I could go to and talk to and bawl my eyes out.

But she had no one like that, and for the very first time in her life she thought of how she had always contrived to shut other people a little away from her.

She had any number of girl friends in town, and very good friends they were, up to a point. But she had never been one for close intimacies, for confiding every secret of her heart in anyone at all. It was as if she had never altogether trusted anyone. When she had become engaged to Kenny, there had been no girl friend with whom she had closeted herself and gushed and enthused about the wonders and joys of loving and of being loved by the right man. So now there was no one to whom she could go, whom she could ask to share her grief with her.

Nor did she really want that.

What, then, did she want?

She didn't quite know. Only not this terrible feeling of aloneness. Not this feeling that nowhere, not anywhere in the town, or even in the whole wide world, was there anyone who really gave a hoot whether she was unhappy or not. Kenny, no doubt, was already dreaming his bright, hopeful dreams about Eileen. Her mother wanted to be kind and was sorry when she was unkind, yet was so completely absorbed in the thoughts of Eileen's homecoming that nothing else mattered a great deal.

And she, Anne, was walking down the street alone. Shut in with her own unhappiness. Too reserved by nature to seek easy companionship with anyone she might happen to run into. And not really wanting that, anyway. Shrinking, instinctively, from the very thought of talking small talk to comparative strangers on this night when the very flesh of her body seemed raw and quivering from the disappointment of seeing her dreams die before her.

She stopped in front of the movie theatre and studied the billboards. It was one of those foolish, farcical comedies, not the sort of thing she ever enjoyed. Tonight she questioned if she could sit through it.

She went on down the street. When she came to Parke's Drug Store, she decided to go in for a soda. It would be something to do, help pass the time. She had found a seat and given her order before she noticed Alex Brooks at the far end of the counter.

He had just finished a coke and was lighting a cigarette.

Seeing her, he smiled, got up and came around to the vacant chair beside her. "I thought you were going fishing," Anne said immediately.

"So did I," said Alex. "Then I thought that I wouldn't go. It was as simple as that." He made a face as the boy set Anne's strawberry soda down in front of her. "How can you drink that revolting mess, anyway?"

Anne laughed. "Oh, it's quite simple. I simply draw on the straw and down it goes."

Alex sighed. "Well, if you didn't have any faults at all, I suppose you wouldn't be human. And if you weren't human, I wouldn't love you. But I'm warning you, woman, when you and I are married, we'll eat together, work together, have fun together, but you'll drink your strawberry sodas alone. There I draw the line."

Anne laughed. "Alex, you fool. You can talk more nonsense."

"Sure I can. Quite a card, this Alex Brooks. The life of every party, the boy in every teen-aged girl's dream of romance. Still we are going to get married, aren't we? Or are we not? I've been restless as a cat all afternoon wondering whether or not I was an engaged guy. Am I, honey? Hmmmm? Am I?"

It was his way, she knew, of asking what had happened with Kenny without putting the question in so many words. She thought, Thank heavens for Alex. For here was one person, after all, to whom she could talk without reservations. She told him, briefly, just what had happened. And when she had finished, he was sensitive enough, understanding enough, not to torment her with maudlin pity, not to prod deeper at the wound with unnecessary questions.

He simply asked her, smiling a little: "So you decided not to use the alibi I offered you."

She shook her head. "Of course I didn't, Alex. You know me better than that, don't you? Do you seriously think I'm the kind who would fall back on a phony engagement just to save my pride?"

He said, not smiling at all now: "You're the one who keeps calling it a phony. I never said that."

"Oh, well, that's what you meant."

"Did I?" He looked around at her, studied her for a moment, then with a slow, quizzical smile he reached in his pocket for a letter and changed the subject.

"Know who Barney Fosdick is?" he asked her.

"Should I know?" The name seemed vaguely familiar, yet Anne couldn't place it immediately until Alex elaborated:

"Barney Fosdick is one of the best portrait painters this country ever turned out. He did several things that got him international recognition. His paintings have brought as much as five thousand bucks. He's getting along in years now. He's well past his prime, and not a well man. Here's a letter I just got from him." And Alex took three or four sheets, written in longhand, from the envelope.

Anne remembered the name now. She asked, surprised: "What in the world is he writing to you about? I've never heard you mention him. Is he an old friend, Alex?"

"Nope." Alex shook his head. "I haven't had the pleasure of meeting the old guy as yet, but I hope to. He's vacationing near here. Doctors sent him south for his health. He's coming over to Hillview one day soon. That's what this letter is about, mostly." Alex was looking over the pages thoughtfully, rereading bits here and there.

"What's bringing him to Hillview?" Anne asked, only faintly curious.

"You," Alex said.

At first Anne didn't grasp what he had said, and when she did, she laughed. She assumed that Alex was kidding her. "Well, now, that's no surprise," she said, her smile droll. "Thing that happens every day in my life. World renowned artists running about, hunting me up. It's my fatal beauty that attracts them, needless to say. Seriously, Alex, what is the man coming here for."

"Just the reason I told you, dear. He wants to see you."

"Oh, Alex, be sensible. You know perfectly well that you're kidding."

He was not kidding. "He saw that picture you modeled for, *Girl In A Yellow Scarf*, at the New York exhibit. He took a fancy to it, same as I did. He also wanted to buy it, only I got my offer in first. Now he wants to make a deal with me. That's partly what this letter is about. The old fellow says he hasn't long to live —bad heart condition. Don't ask me why he's taken such a fancy to the picture; I only know what he's written here and he didn't go into reasons. Maybe it reminds him of his first sweetheart or something. Anyway, he very much wants to have it to live with for as long as he does live. He wants me to let him have it, with the understanding that it's to be turned back to me when he dies. That's what he's coming over to Hillview to talk with me about."

Alex turned to the last page, studying it for a moment before he read, quoting: "If it can possibly be arranged, I should deem it a great privilege to become personally acquainted with the young lady who modeled for this exceptionally fine piece."

Alex folded the letter. "Expresses himself like a gentleman of the old school, doesn't he? Well, what about it, Anne? Have I your permission to bring the old bird around when he gets here?"

"Why, certainly. It would be wonderful to meet anyone so famous and a real artist. Only I just can't think why he should want to meet me."

"Good," said Alex. "Then that's all settled." Then, with another of his abrupt changes of subject: "I'm going fishing tomorrow, Anne. No fooling, this time. Just for the day. How would you like to go along?"

A little surprised at the invitation, Anne laughed. "But I don't know how to fish."

"Who cares? I'll teach you, if you'd like to learn. If not, we'll just sit by a mountain stream and watch the pretty little fish swim by. We'll consider the relative value of fish in the general scheme of things, as compared with man. Personally, my vote is for the fish. We'll forget our troubles. With your permission, I'll take along a book of poetry and read to you, just to give a romantic touch to our little outing. You didn't know that I was a poetry lover? Ah, Anne, my girl, the things you don't know about me! Incidentally, we might take along some bottles of pop and some sandwiches. Some such little feast is in order, since it happens to be my birthday, and if you ask me which birthday, I shall take it as gross impertinence. I expect to feel about eighteen, with you sitting beside me on the river bank, and you will look about sixteen. So just let's say that eighteen is going a-wooing sixteen, and leave it at that, shall we?"

He said earnestly: "Will you come with me, Anne? Please."

She looked at him, and for no accountable reason her eyes were swimming. She had been longing for some-one, someone she could feel close to and free with, some-one to ease her inner loneliness. And here he was. Alex. He seemed a kind of refuge. A sweet, comforting refuge. And remembering suddenly his kiss on her mouth, a vaguely exciting refuge, too.

She said: "Of course I'll come, Alex. I'll love it."

CHAPTER 7

After half a dozen more telegrams, and as many last minute changes of plan, Eileen finally arrived the following Monday morning. At the station Aunt Molly and Uncle Ned were already waiting when Anne and her mother drove up in their old sedan, vintage 1938. Uncle Ned, stout, cheerful, and secretly thankful for a heart condition which gave him an excuse to avoid all physical exertion, even walking, conceded with a chuckle that not for anything would he have missed the show of Eileen's arrival. A few casual friends had collected on the wooden platform outside the small red brick station building. The news of Eileen's return had already spread all over town. Nellie had given out the story that Eileen, suffering from a "nervous condition," was under doctor's orders to come home for a "long rest."

The train, as was expected, was seven or eight minutes late. It always was. It was a junction train, carrying only day coaches, which connected with the express from Chicago and stopped at every way station.

It came, finally.

Two or three passengers got off. Then after a brief pause, during which everything and everyone—the puffing engine, the trainman, the porter, the waiting relatives, and especially Nellie—seemed to be waiting in a state of suspended animation, Eileen appeared, smiling and waving, on the train platform. She was descending the train steps, flanked to the front and rear by two young men wearing the uniforms of marine officers.

Eileen was fairly tall and dark, with a rich, exotic type of beauty. Her smile was as dazzling and seemed as practiced, which it was, as that of a screen star. And her every movement as graceful. She was wearing a gray suit which had an outrageously expensive look. She was wearing a red hat, red accouterments, and over one arm she carried a leopard skin coat.

"Mother, darling!" Eileen threw herself into her mother's arms, and when she withdrew there were tears in her eyes. She had always cried easily and beautifully.

There were even a few tears left for her greeting of Anne. "Oh, darling, it's so wonderful to see you, so wonderful to see all of you." And her outstretched arms seemed to embrace everyone. "And so heavenly to be home again. I can't tell you."

Then she remembered the boy friends, waiting in the background. Catching an arm of each, she presented them to her mother, to Anne. Captain Ed Stoneleigh,

Lieutenant Walter Connor. They were to be stationed at Fort Prendle. To the captain, with an arch smile and still clinging to his arm: "During the last war, the boys out at Fort Prendle said I rated a medal or something for my work as a morale builder."

The captain smiled, said as was expected of him: "If you ask me, this is the same old war, and I feel my morale slipping badly. Can I count on you to take care of it for me?"

"Now there," Eileen retorted gaily, "is the answer to something that's been bothering me. My *real* reason for coming back to Hillview. All because there had to be someone to take care of your poor little morale. Captain, would you care to bring along your morale and have dinner with us this evening? And you, too, Lieutenant Connor. In other words," another gay laugh, "I know mother will adore feeding my old pals, Ed and Walt, and so will I. And if you should bring along an itch to go dancing later, it won't make me mad."

Once they were in the car, with Anne driving, Nellie was faintly reproachful. "I don't mean to be critical, dear. But I rather wish you hadn't been quite so free and easy with those young officers. You know how quick people are to talk. You're supposed to be still a married woman. I haven't let anyone know that you're divorcing Bob. But if you start right in—"

"Well, I'm not divorcing Bob," Eileen stated unexpectedly.

"You're not? Why, I thought you wrote—"

"I know," Eileen said. "I did write that I'd made up my mind to get a divorce. Bob had been getting on my nerves. I really didn't see how I could stand any more of it. But we talked things over. Bob begged and pleaded with me not to do anything too hastily. So finally I promised him that I wouldn't."

She laughed. "Bob says that what I need is a vacation from marriage. He thinks I got married too soon, before I was really ready to settle down to being married. He said once that I should have gone on playing with dolls another year or two, and he could be right, at that. Anyway, he told me to come on home and just forget that I had a husband. He told me to go dancing, have fun, find some new boy friends, or go back to the old ones if I wanted to. I'm to feel as free as a bird, and simply forget that he exists.

"Of course," Eileen added as a careless afterthought. "Bob is to feel free to have other girl friends if he likes. Only," that throaty, amused laugh again, "I don't have any worries on that score. Bob never looks at another girl. He just isn't the type."

Nellie looked worried. All this struck her as a very curious attitude for a young husband to take. She had been all in favor of a legal separation, if that was what

Eileen wanted. But, "Are you very sure that Bob isn't interested in someone else, dear?"

Eileen shook her head emphatically. "Not a chance. The lad is crazier about me than he ever was. He was willing to do anything, agree to anything, to keep me from getting a divorce. I've been so terribly bored lately. Bob works so hard, sometimes he has to work nights, and I'm left alone so much. I get so restless I simply can't stand it. Messing around a little apartment all the time simply drives me mad. And Bob doesn't like me to go out on the street alone after dark. He says it worries him so he can't get any work done."

Nellie said, surprised: "But all this sounds so different from what you wrote in your letter, Eileen. You said that Bob had been cruel and unkind."

"Did I?" said Eileen, the lift of her beautifully arched dark brows suggesting that she hadn't the faintest recollection of ever having written such a thing. "Oh, well, it was probably the mood I was in. No, I can't honestly say that Bob was ever what you'd call cruel to me, unless you want to call it cruelty to leave me sitting around by myself, getting so bored I could scream."

"Are you still in love with Bob?" Nellie asked.

Eileen, faintly amused at the question, gave a pretty shrug. "I wouldn't know, Mother. I really wouldn't. I don't go all trembly when I hear his feet pattering along the hall, if that's what you mean. I'm still rather fond of the character. But am I fond enough of him to go on spending the rest of my life with him? That's the sixty-four dollar question. Personally, I doubt it. But I promised him to give the thing a chance. So that's the setup. I'm vacationing from marriage. If I get bored with my vacation, I'll go back to Chicago and Bob. If something better turns up, I'll go to Reno."

Her voice turned surprisingly sharp. "Meanwhile, I mean to do exactly what I said, Mother. I mean to have a good time. If I want to invite men to the house and go out with them, I mean to do it. And I'm just not interested in what the meddling Matties around this hick town may think about it. So that's the way it's going to be, Mother. And if you don't approve—"

Her curt tone made the words a kind of subtle threat. Nellie, always ready to give in where Eileen was concerned, said quickly: "Now Eileen, pet, you know that I want you to do whatever you think best, whatever will make for your ultimate happiness. I promise you that I shan't try to interfere. I just didn't understand at first. Your letters had given me a rather different impression of what the situation was. But now that you've explained everything—"

To Anne's way of thinking, Eileen had explained nothing, except that she was as self-centered as ever, that she was concerned more with amusing herself than with her responsibility toward Bob who was working hard to get ahead, that now she had run away from her home and her marriage, as a child would play hookey from school, to discover if there wasn't something more interesting to be found on the outside.

She was taking advantage of Bob's deep and thoroughly unselfish love for her. No man, Anne knew, could enjoy the idea of having his wife go home to stay indefinitely, to amuse herself, go dancing, go on other dates with as many new or old boy friends as happened to strike her fancy. Yet Bob, because of his love for Eileen, was ready to stand for it. And Eileen, completely irresponsible, hadn't a qualm about taking advantage of that unselfish love.

Anne felt sick at heart, sick in spirit. It was because of this completely selfish and undeniably lovely creature that she, Anne, had had to relinquish her own love. No doubt Kenny would find himself head over heels in love with Eileen again the minute he saw her. For she was more beautiful than ever.

Eyes intent on her driving, Anne had taken no part in the conversation. They were in sight of the house when Eileen turned to her, laughing. "Well, Anne darling, I see you're the same quiet little mouse as always. Still waters run deep, so I'm told. It's positively frightening to think what a deep one you must be."

Anne smiled. "I'm not too good a driver. I just can't

talk and watch out for traffic at the same time."

"What a safe and sane little darling you are." Eileen's pretty laughter had a gurgling sound. "I'll bet you wouldn't dream of trying to play married and single both at the same time, the way I'm doing."

"No. I probably wouldn't."

"Good. That's my play-it-safe, solemn-eyed little sister. What a lot of trouble you'll save yourself, being the way you are. But of course you'll miss a lot of fun, too. By the way, darling, how's the big romance coming along? I might as well confess that I'm jealous. Imagine you getting yourself engaged to Kenny Wilcox. It seems only yesterday that the lad was the favorite dream boy in my life. When I see Kenny, I must give him a good scolding for his faithlessness to me."

Anne's smile was cool, her voice under perfect control. "I'm afraid you won't have anything to scold him about, Eileen. Kenny and I aren't engaged."

Eileen's beautiful dark eyes widened, for the first time showing an interest that was more than perfunctory. "You aren't? But, Anne, you wrote me a few weeks ago that—"

"That was a few weeks ago."

"Oh. I see. You mean you've broken off with him since you wrote?"

"Yes." Anne nodded. Then, attempting a rather poor joke, she laughed: "It seems to be Kenny's fate to be jilted by the Veigh girls. Lucky for him there aren't any more of us."

Eileen's eyes had taken on an extremely thoughtful expression. She smiled, but not very much, over Anne's facetious comment. "So you and Kenny aren't engaged, after all," she repeated, as if it were a definitely interesting item of news. "Who broke it off?" she asked suddenly. "You? Or Kenny?"

Thoroughly provoked at Eileen for keeping on the subject, Anne was tempted to tell her it was none of her business. Then, changing her mind, she decided to let Eileen have the truth straight between the eyes. "I broke it off," Anne said, "when I learned that you were coming home. There seems to be some doubt as to whether Kenny still nurses a hopeless passion for you, or whether he doesn't. I decided to turn him loose so he could find out."

You could tell by the sparkle in her eyes and the quick lift in her voice that Eileen was thrilled and delighted to hear all this. "You mean to tell me that Kenny is still in love with me? Why, the poor darling."

"I didn't tell you anything of the sort," Anne said crisply. I told you that he didn't know and neither do I."

"Doesn't it amount to the same thing?" Eileen asked sweetly.

It would not, Anne realized, be a loving, sisterly gesture to turn around and slap Eileen in the face. There were the amenities to be observed, so Anne tried to observe them.

Anne said sweetly: "I have Kenny's phone number written down on a card for you. He is usually in his office until four o'clock, and he's very good at giving shots to people who are in a highly nervous condition. You did say that your nerves were shot, didn't you, sis? So if I were you, right after we have lunch, I'd phone Kenny and make an appointment. I'd go over to his office and have him give me a shot. Then you can ask him if he's still hopelessly in love with you. I really believe that's the best way of finding out. Now, if you don't mind, shall we stop discussing it?"

"Now, Anne," her mother put in, "you mustn't be so touchy. Eileen is only trying to show a sisterly interest in your affairs."

"Of course I am," Eileen echoed swiftly. "I've been away so long, and I love you all so much, and it's so very wonderful to be home with my own mother and sister again, I was just truly and sincerely interested in how your love affair was going. I didn't mean to pry, Anne. Heavens! I hope you don't think I'm still carrying a torch for Kenny. I was just trying to be sisterly."

Oh, sure, Anne thought, gritting her teeth. Sisterly Eileen. Where Kenny was concerned, or any other attractive man for that matter, she was about as sisterly as a nice, hungry rattlesnake slowly uncoiling before it struck for blood.

Then, quickly ashamed of that thought, Anne reminded herself, I'm jealous. That's all that's wrong with me. I'm just plain, everyday jealous, because Eileen is so beautiful and has a kind of charm that I haven't got.

Perhaps she was unkind and altogether wrong in thinking that Eileen would get right out to get Kenny back, if for no other reason than to please her vanity by proving that she could do it.

But let me not be overcome by all these impulses of sweetness and light, Anne thought grimly. Because she knew perfectly well that she wasn't wrong. Eileen would be on the phone, calling Kenny, the minute she could invent a graceful and plausible excuse. If not today, then tomorrow.

It was, after all, today. Only Eileen didn't bother with phoning. She simply went straight to Kenny's office. That very afternoon.

CHAPTER 8

By the end of the week, it was hard to realize that Eileen had ever been away. Just as in the old days, the house seemed to revolve around Eileen and Eileen's activities. When the phone rang, as it did constantly, it was usually for Eileen. Old friends calling her up. Someone giving a party. Could she come? And in the evenings, officers from Fort Prendle ringing her up to go dancing, to go to a show, or just to meet them and drive around. Through the captain and the lieutenant, whom she had met on the train, Eileen had already met a score of other men at the base. Some of them took her for a single girl. Others, having heard a sketchy account of how she was "on vacation" from her husband, felt a heightened interest for this very reason. In less than a week Eileen already had more dates on hand than she could handle. She loved it all. How she loved it!

Exactly what was going on between Eileen and Kenny, Anne didn't know. For outside of a few vague remarks which told exactly nothing, Eileen was keeping mum on that subject.

Because Kenny's reception of Eileen had been a little less enthusiastic than she had expected? Or just the opposite?

Had their old feeling for each other come back to such sharp and urgent life that even Eileen, who usually babbled so freely about all of her affairs, wanted to keep this very special thing to herself?

She had freely admitted going to his office that first afternoon. "That was a great idea you had, Anne. I did need a shot for my nerves."

They had lunched together the next day. Eileen, laughing: "I practically had to drag the lad by the hair of his head. I said, Darling, I'm the first sweetheart you ever had and I consider it your moral duty to take me to lunch when I'm just home. Funny Kenny. He seemed to have some foolish scruples about taking a married gal to lunch. And us such old friends."

From there on Eileen gave nothing away. If they were meeting each other on the side, Eileen wasn't telling. She simply looked very mysterious whenever Kenny's name came up and said nothing. Her attitude seemed to be that they could make what they liked out of it.

Anne, for her part, wanted to make nothing of it. She wanted only, with all of her heart, to forget the whole thing. To forget Kenny in so far as it was possible. Because only by forgetting him could she ever hope to forget that dull, dark pain which never quite left off clawing at her heart. She had never been so thankful that she had a job to keep her busy. And with every passing day, she was more and more thankful that she had Alex to fall back on, as a friend as well as an employer.

Their day's outing together had been a complete success. Alex had proved himself an ideal companion. His conversation was intelligent and stimulating without being stuffy. He could discuss world problems from the angle of a man who had read widely and thoughtfully. He had an appreciation of poetry and all of the artistic phases of life. And he could be as gay and prankish and full of fun as a fourteen-year-old youngster.

Anne had had a far better time that day than she would have believed possible. While not forgetting that her dearest hopes and dreams had, only the day before, been blown to bits, Alex, in some very subtle way, made her feel that life had not ended altogether. Even this soon she was able to laugh, to take a real interest when Alex actually did give her her first instruction in casting a line, in waiting quietly and patiently for a fish to come swimming along and rise to the bait. "Fishing is a great lesson in patience," Alex told her.

Even this soon she was able to feel that at least one day had ended all too soon.

After that day, it was inevitable that a more personal

note should be injected into their office relationship. Yet this again was such a subtle change that Anne could not have said in so many words exactly what the difference was. For her part, she seemed to be working harder than ever, partly because a sudden rush of work had come in, and even more, because she welcomed work. The more she could lose herself in what she was doing, the oftener she could go home evenings, so exhausted both mentally and physically that she could scarcely see straight. This gave her less time for brooding and feeling sorry for herself.

After Eileen's return, Anne fell more and more into the habit of working evenings. Her excuse to Nellie, who considered such devotion to a silly old office job complete nonsense, was that there were so many interruptions during the day. Clients, who were old friends as well, tactlessly insisted upon sitting around for a personal chat. They interfered with her schedule. She would never get caught up unless she went back to the office evenings.

Nellie would say: "Well, I think Alex Brooks ought to be ashamed of himself, piling more work on you than you're able to do. It strikes me that he's using you for a good thing, Anne." And: "Eileen feels the way you're acting, Anne. It looks as if you're deliberately staying away from the house as much as possible because she's here."

Which, of course, was perfectly true.

Eileen started right in having a crowd in every evening. The captain and the lieutenant brought around other officers from the base. Girls must be found for them, so Eileen would phone old friends, after first inviting Anne to join the party and getting turned down.

Eileen put it up to her mother: "What's wrong with Anne? Honestly, she doesn't act human. You'd think she'd like to meet some good-looking men and go dancing. What's she sore about?"

Nellie would shake her head vaguely. "Anne is such a strange person. Always one for keeping to herself. She's never been one for mixing very much."

"Well," Eileen would pout, "I think it's a funny way to act. I want to include her in things and she won't give me any cooperation."

Which was one of the things that annoyed Anne vaguely. Eileen was willing to include her. When she had an extra, not too attractive man on hand and didn't know what to do about him, she was generously willing to turn him over to Anne.

The belle of the ball was graciously willing to throw a few spare crumbs to her less popular, less attractive sister.

Perhaps Eileen didn't intend it that way.

Perhaps it was a kind of childish pique on Anne's part—a faint envy. Anne knew that this could be true.

She was not proud of herself if it was true.

Still, why weary herself with dates that bored her?

Why go dancing with strange men in whom she had no interest, prod herself to a false gaiety, when in actuality she was bored stiff, force herself to stay up until all hours when what she really wanted was to be in bed getting her rest? All of it meant taking something out of her, eating up just that much more of her energy, and left her weary and scarcely fit for work when morning came.

She did try it just once. It was a deadly evening. But Eileen told her: "I should think you'd be thrilled. A dance at the officers' club. And what was wrong with that Major Hilton?"

There had been nothing at all wrong with Major Hilton except that in dancing, he stumbled all over Anne's feet and he seemed allergic to all forms of conversation except wise-cracks. Anne had crawled wearily into bed around four o'clock. She awoke, late, with a splitting headache—the first headache she had had in years. "I'm sorry, sis, but you'll have to include me out," she said, the next time Eileen suggested a similar date.

"Simply not the party type, eh?" was Alex's grinning comment. He saw and understood more than he let on. This, no doubt, had something to do with his suggestion that Anne stay downtown and have dinner with him on the evenings when she planned to work after hours.

"You'll be doing me a favor," he assured her. "Don't you imagine a guy gets sick and tired of eating by himself, evening after evening?"

And furthermore, he added mischievously, if he fell back on one or another of the town's glamour girls for a dinner companion, it was likely to be misinterpreted as a proposal of marriage. He had simply had to school himself to eating alone. But, confidentially, he had never learned to like it.

"You aren't afraid," Anne teased him, "that after one or two dinners at a drive-in, I'll demand to know your intentions?"

"But I've already told you my intentions, honey. Trouble is, you won't take me seriously. However, if you remain steadfast in your refusal to lead me up to the altar, maybe you'll at least break down and accompany me to an occasional movie. Just to relieve the intolerable loneliness. Ah, Anne, the unspeakable loneliness of a bachelor's existence. The emptiness of it all. Anne, Anne, if you only realized."

One day, when he had been joking like this, Anne said laughingly: "Oh, Alex, shut up with such crazy talk. If you don't, I'll shut you up one of these times by taking you seriously. Then what?"

"Why not try it and find out?" Alex suggested.

Anne sighed. "I'd probably find myself out of a job. You'd get the cold jitters if you thought that I—"

Alex inquired with his slow, quizzical smile: "Has it ever occurred to you, my girl, that you aren't quite as smart as you think you are?"

"I don't think I'm the least bit smart," Anne had retorted. "On the contrary. Sometimes it occurs to me that I'm the world's worst dope."

Which, as she confided to Alex, was the way she felt about the party. "Speak of it in capitals and in a hushed and reverent tone," she told Alex wryly. "And kindly spare my feelings and don't remind me that it was to have been the party to announce my engagement."

She realized belatedly that she should have called the whole thing off, once she had broken off things with Kenny. But she had already let it be known that she was giving a big party. Fortunately, she had not told anyone that she was planning to make a formal announcement of her engagement that night. Thus she was spared the humiliation of retraction. It was her mother who had suggested brightly: "I think we should go right on with plans for a party, dear. Only now we can call it a homecoming party for Eileen."

Which made little difference to Anne. She cared less than nothing about what kind of a party they called it. Her only wish was that she could think up some plausible excuse not to be there. She asked Alex: "My poor little engagement party folded up and died. Now the party is all Eileen's show. Alex, couldn't you invent a

nice business trip for me? Don't you have a case that
needs urgent, first-hand attention say, out in California?
Or the Fiji Islands would do even better."

Then, completely honest: "Alex, I'm a coward! I
don't want to be in on that party. There's be a ghost
there, and I always was afraid of ghosts."

Alex grinned at her. "Well, if you weren't such a
little Puritan, I could take you out that night and get
you drunk. Or if you would only take my adoration
seriously, we could get married and show up late at the
party to announce our marriage. Think how that would
startle the natives. That, I think, would even get a rise
out of that prima-donna sister of yours. These two
courses are open to you, dear. From there on, my inven-
tive ingenuity fails me. So I'm afraid you'll just have to
face the music. And cheer up. Maybe it won't be as bad
as you think."

"Will you come, Alex? I know you hate that kind of
party. But please come anyway. Please come and be my
escort. I need somebody just for myself," she added des-
perately. "Eileen will have a raft of officers swarming
around her. She's planning to invite practically the whole
of the officers' club."

Alex said sure, he'd come, if she wanted him to. And
he said again, in the usual humorous tone that went with
the suggestion he had made so often that it was becoming laughable: "You could still make it an engagement

party, you know. If you wanted to announce your engagement to me."

Then, more seriously, he asked her if she expected Kenny to show up at the party. Anne said that she didn't know. She supposed that Eileen would see to it that Kenny came, although she hadn't as yet mentioned it. Anne was pretty sure that Eileen was seeing Kenny, although her sister made a point of not mentioning him. If Kenny's name came up, Eileen's mask came down. But there were plenty of ways that they could meet quietly, without anyone knowing. Anne's guess was that they were meeting occasionally, but that Kenny didn't want it known. After all, Eileen was still a married woman and Kenny had his professional reputation to consider. Furthermore, Kenny was by nature a scrupulous person with great integrity and a sense of honor.

Anne doubted that he could bring himself to see very much of Eileen as long as she was legally bound to another man. But an occasional meeting, enough to talk and decide how they still felt about each other, was possible. "Oh, I think so," Anne said. "I don't know for sure, but I think so. And I'm sure that Eileen will see to it that Kenny comes to her party."

Because, by now, it was Eileen's party in every sense. Nellie, talking over some preparation, would say: "Now about your party, Eileen. Do you think we should have this or that?"

Already, Eileen had postponed it a week from the date Anne had originally set. Now it was set for the next Saturday night. Eileen had needed more time to select a new dress, although her bags, brought from Chicago, were overflowing with beautiful clothes.

But what was a party without a brand-new dress?

She had decided on turquoise blue. Then, changing her mind, she decided that dead white with emerald green ornaments would be the thing. Then, discarding both ideas as not at all what she wanted, she had made a hurried trip to Washington and brought home a flame-colored taffeta which was, Anne thought, the most daring dress she had ever seen.

Without question, it was stunning on Eileen with her rich, dark beauty. Also, without question, not a man would know that any other girl was present. Once Eileen appeared in that dress every other woman would look hopelessly washed out.

I might just as well wear a cotton house dress for all the attention anyone will pay to me, thought Anne. And she had a great notion to do it.

She still wished that she could invent some last minute excuse to leave town when the day came. And maybe she would have, if Alex hadn't shamed her out of it. "Do you want anyone to think that you're the kind who runs away because you can't take it?"

"Who would think that?" Anne demanded. "Who

would know?"

"You would," Alex reminded her, very gently.

And he was right, of course.

Eileen who, all her life, had loved getting ready to give a party, could do nothing but talk party, party, party for days before the appointed night.

She took all the preparations into her own hands. With good reason, to be sure. Since Anne remained completely indifferent, explaining that she had too much work at the office to allow her any spare time for party preparations. "Aren't you even going to get a new dress?" Eileen asked her, looking slightly shocked when Anne retorted: "Why should I?"

"Well, what are you going to wear?"

Anne said that she hadn't any idea. Whatever was closest to hand, she supposed, when she opened her closet that night. "It's your party, dear. All of these officers who will be coming are your friends. You are the one who wants to impress them. As for our old friends," Anne laughed, "they, too, will be looking at you. They won't know what I have on."

A remark which caused Eileen to offer what she considered a valuable piece of advice. To her mind, this was the thing that every girl should learn, if she wasn't born knowing it. "Anne, darling, hasn't anyone ever told you? You should make people notice what you have on. Any girl can make people sit up and take notice if she works at it." She had added, sweetly condescending: "You know, Anne, you aren't really bad-looking. You have a few really good points, your eyes for instance. You should get yourself up to accentuate them. Only you don't. You don't do a thing for yourself."

Anne thanked her, laughing, for this faint praise. And for the advice which, unfortunately, came a little late. Certainly too late to do anything about it for the party.

Anne said: "It's your show, Eileen. It's all yours. I'll appear in my usual role of the mousey little sister, and I'm not feeling sorry for myself, Eileen. And I'm not trying to work up any role of martyr, either. Please don't say that. It isn't true. I'm simply awfully busy these days and I've never cared as much for parties as you do, anyway."

Thoroughly annoyed—and for what reason Anne couldn't fathom—Eileen said shortly: "If you tell me you'd rather go up to your room and read a good book, I'll scream. Honestly, Anne, sometimes I think all of this shy and retiring air is an act with you. You've been overdoing it just a little, if you ask me. Don't you like it that I've come home? Do you resent my being here?"

Anne was quickly conciliatory. Nothing was farther from her mind than to hurt Eileen's feelings, and she said so. "I don't resent your being here and I am not putting on any act. I haven't been any too gay since you came. That I'll admit. I don't think we need go into the reasons."

"I suppose you mean because of Kenny," Eileen said sharply. "Well, you needn't blame me for that. Did I ask you to break off your engagement? Did I?"

"Oh, please," Anne said quickly. "Let's not talk about that. Let's just leave Kenny out of this, if you don't mind. I can't see what he has to do with whether or not I'm getting a new dress for your party. Please, Eileen, let's skip it. Okay?"

And that was that, for the moment.

Eileen went on with her excited preparations. She had insisted on arranging for a small orchestra for the dance music, which even Nellie conceded seemed a needless expense. "After all, dear, we're very small town and this is supposed to be an informal welcome home party." But Eileen overrode that objection, just as she overrode doubts about bringing in a caterer to provide the refreshments. "Look, Mother, when I give a party, I like to do it right. I'll pay for all of this myself if you can't afford it. Just because the Hillview natives aren't used to sophisticated parties is no reason why I shouldn't give one. Frankly, I want to knock their eyes out. And furthermore," Eileen added, "some of those boys at the base are anything but hicks. Some of those lads come from wealthy homes and they know how things should be done."

"Eileen, believe me, darling, I don't want to seem critical. But why should you care what those boys think? I dare say many of them are very nice young men, and used to seeing things done right. However, you seem to forget about Bob, dear. And it worries me. If you and Bob—"

But Eileen, stamping her angry little red-shod foot, had wanted to hear nothing about Bob. "I've told you, Mother. I'm on vacation from Bob. I want to have a good time and I want this party to be right. I mean to have it right. And I can't see that it makes the slightest difference about my loyalty to Bob, or my wifely duty to Bob, whether I give this party with or without the trimmings.".

So Eileen meant to give it with all the trimmings.

It was three or four days before the all-important Saturday night that the name of a certain Andy Ritter, a colonel by rank, began to enter into Eileen's conversations.

Eileen mentioned him, the first time, at breakfast. She had met the colonel the night before at another informal dance at the officers' club. "The lad is tall, blond, and handsome," Eileen enthused. And, she added, a Texan. On first meeting, he appeared to be the grim and silent type. But just give her time, Eileen assured them, and she was sure she could soften him up. "There's a rumor," she added, "that the lad has more money than he knows what to do with. Oil wells." She had invited him to her party, threatening to skip out to the camp and drag him in by his scalp if he didn't come on his own steam.

Anne said, unable to resist the mild dig: "Well, well. A millionaire and a colonel. This bodes no good for Bob. Perhaps I'd better write my brother-in-law and warn him to expect the worst." Having said the words with a teasing grin, she was astonished at Eileen's angry flare-up.

"Look, Anne, if I catch you meddling in my affairs or writing things to Bob that are none of your business, I'll make you wish you hadn't."

It was not the first time that Eileen's attitude about Bob had puzzled Anne, nor the first time that she had wondered if Eileen had told the whole truth about that situation. Could it possibly be that Eileen's "vacation" from marriage was an enforced vacation? That their temporary separation was Bob's idea, not Eileen's?

Her sister, Anne knew very well, had always been quick to invent little "fairy stories" to present her own doings in the best possible light. Had there been trouble with Bob, with Bob laying down the law? Eileen, if she ran true to form, would be the last one to tell anything that put her in a bad light. Or even in a dim one.

Oh, well, it was none of her business, Anne reminded herself. If Eileen was staging a little play—casting herself as the star, or the wronged wife, or what have you—let her stage and direct it according to her own ideas. It made little difference to Anne. And to Kenny?

Ultimately, Anne was forced to come back to Kenny in her thoughts.

With absolutely nothing to go on, she simply couldn't turn off the fantasies which would come to torment her every so often. They were most frequent just before she fell off to sleep at night.

She had deliberately avoided Kenny ever since the day when she had returned his ring. He had not been near the house, nor had he phoned Anne, either at home or at the office. Perhaps could she have seen him, just once, she would have known just what his feelings were in relation to herself and to Eileen.

Not knowing, she had only her imagination to go on and her imagination ran riot. She would lie with closed eyes, imagining the scene between them, that first day when Eileen went to his office. She pictured Kenny taking Eileen into his arms. Looking deep into her beautiful eyes, slowly putting his lips to her soft, bright ones. Whispering thickly: "Darling, oh my darling, it's been so long. I've tried to forget you but I never could. You are my real love. You always will be. I just can't help myself."

And after that?

Were they meeting clandestinely? It would be a simple enough matter, Anne knew. Eileen had the use of the family car, and frequently she took it out in the evenings with only the vaguest explanations as to where she was going. Nor did she discuss afterwards where she had been.

Hillview was within easy driving distance of three or four other small towns where there were quiet, secluded little restaurants where no one would ever see them. Oh, it would be simple enough to arrange, and no one would ever know.

Kenny. It would be exactly like him to say: "I must see you, talk with you occasionally, but not too often. Because to have you near me, where I can look at you, talk with you, touch you simply by reaching out my hand—I can't stand too much of that, darling. It's sweet torment, but torment just the same. So until you've made up your mind what you're going to do about Bob—until you are really and in fact free—we must content ourselves with these very occasional meetings."

Oh, that would be Kenny, all right. That would be the way he would handle things. His sense of right and wrong was too strong ever to permit him to indulge in any easy, obvious flirtation with a girl who, legally, still belonged to another man.

And if this were not the truth, why wouldn't Kenny have phoned her long before now?

If, when he saw Eileen again, he had discovered that his old feeling for her was completely dead, Kenny would have been on the phone in no time flat. "Darling, this is a completely free man who is calling you, and when do I see you?" Of course that was what he would have done.

But she hadn't heard a word. Not one single word from him. And since Eileen seemed resolved to give away nothing where Kenny was concerned, Anne had given up trying to feel her out.

Then, the very last night before the party, Eileen pulled another surprise. She had gone out to a movie, alone so she said. She had come in before eleven o'clock. Anne was in bed, just ready to turn off the lamp on her bedside table, when Eileen opened her door, not bothering to knock. She closed the door carefully behind her. Then, coming over to the bed, she looked at Anne. Anne saw that she was furious. Her mouth was working and her hands were clenched.

What's up now? Anne wondered.

She couldn't have been more surprised than when she heard Eileen saying: "You needn't think that I don't know you've told Kenny not to come to my party tomorrow night. And I think it's a mean, contemptible trick. You don't want him yourself, because you've fallen in love with Alex Brooks. That's plain enough. But I guess you aren't sure of landing Alex, so you've thought up this neat little scheme to keep Kenny dangling. Break your engagement on the pretext that I'm coming home, but when I get here, put on this act of injured innocence. So Kenny is afraid to move or turn for fear it isn't being fair to you. As clever a little act as I've ever seen—playing both ends against the middle. But I think you're mean, mean, mean, to keep Kenny from coming to my party."

With that, Eileen dissolved into tears.

For a moment, all Anne could do was stare at her. Finally she managed the only words she could think of. "Are you absolutely crazy?"

CHAPTER 9

Anne was so weary that her bones ached, and nervously tense from her physical exhaustion. She had had a busy day, and another one ahead of her—with the dreaded party at the end of it. All she wanted was to be allowed to turn out the lights and go to sleep. She was definitely in no mood to put up with one of Eileen's tantrums. Eileen's little outburst had been so absurd, the things she said so completely divorced from all reality, that it would have been laughable had Anne been less physically depleted.

But, tired as she was, she simply wasn't up to humoring her sister who had never struck her as more of a spoiled baby.

Anne heard herself saying, more sharply than she had intended: "Look, Eileen, I need my sleep. If Kenny won't come to your party, that's too bad. But to say that it's my fault is simply silly. I haven't seen Kenny or talked to him since you came home. And as for saying that I'm in love with Alex, if you don't mind my asking, how did you ever dream up *that* crazy idea?" She laughed. "Alex isn't the marrying kind and everyone in town knows it. I work in his office, and we're friends. But I assure you it's strictly a platonic friendship."

Eileen laughed shortly. "Platonic friendship! The old, old alibi. Maybe it will be news to you, darling, to hear that there ain't no such thing—not with any attractive, unmarried man. And here's another piece of news. It's town talk that you're in love with the lad and that Alex is slipping fast. But have it your own way, if you insist. Only don't expect me to believe you. However, I didn't come in here to discuss Alex Brooks. It's Kenny and my party."

Anne, sitting up, had shoved an extra pillow behind her back. She inquired, honestly curious: "Whatever gave you the idea that I was keeping Kenny away from your party?"

Eileen, looking sulky, had curled up at the foot of the bed, one foot tucked under her. Apparently she was going to stay, whether Anne liked it or not, until she got good and ready to go back to her own room. "He practically told me so," she said.

"I don't believe it," Anne stated flatly, after a moment's silence. "Kenny doesn't lie."

"Well, maybe he didn't say that in so many words. Yet he did say definitely that he wouldn't come, and any nitwit could figure out that you're the reason."

Anne shrugged. "No doubt he thinks that it wouldn't be in very good taste. After all—"

"Well, good taste or not, I want Kenny at my party."

"Why?"

The direct impact of that one brief word seemed to startle Eileen momentarily. "Why shouldn't I want him to come?" she countered sullenly. "After all, Kenny Wilcox and I grew up together. When we were kids, we always went to each other's parties. Then we fell in love."

"Then you married another man," Anne reminded her sharply. "For heaven's sake, Eileen, aren't you ever going to grow up? Are you never going to find out that you can't eat your cake and have it too? I don't know whether you're still in love with Kenny or not. If you are, you should divorce Bob. If you're not, if Bob is the one you honestly want—"

She sighed, shaking her head. "It's hard to make you out, Eileen. I don't mean to criticize. It's your own business how you want to manage your life. But the way it looks to me, you won't play honest with anyone. You're still married to Bob, but before you were home twenty-four hours, you were rushing around on other dates, arranging for parties, making a play for Kenny, doing exactly as you did before you ever had a husband. And all that talk about Bob sending you off on a vacation from marriage, you can't expect anyone to take that without a grain of salt, Eileen. A man doesn't order the wife he loves to run off and have herself a gay time with other men. He just doesn't."

"Bob did," Eileen said. Then, to Anne's astonishment, Eileen had thrown herself across the bed and was sobbing wildly.

To Anne's further astonishment, Eileen was sobbing out a story that was not, after all, too surprising. The surprising thing was that Eileen was, for once, admitting the real truth.

Bob too, it seemed, had accused Eileen of being a spoiled baby. Of refusing to grow up and accept the responsibilities of married life. "He's like everyone else," Eileen cried brokenly. "When we were first married, he spoiled me and pampered me. He used to call me his spoiled beautiful doll and said he loved me for being just the way I was. Then the change came almost overnight. He seemed to hate me for being that way. It's always been like that. People spoil me; then they blame me for being spoiled."

Something to that, Anne admitted to herself wryly. For every spoiled brat, there had to be someone to do the spoiling.

"Even you, Anne," Eileen was saying. "You've always taken a back seat when I was around, and you did it again when you knew I was coming home. Nobody asked you to break your engagement to Kenny because of me. You just turned him loose as if it were the natural thing to do. Why didn't you fight for him, if you thought a fight was indicated? But no. You just open your hands and let him go. Then you blame me for it."

"I'm not blaming you," Anne said gently.

"Oh, yes you do. Maybe you don't know it yourself, but in your heart you blame me, all right. And you've resented my being here. You keep out of my way. You're either so darned polite to me that it's painful or else you don't pay any attention to me at all."

Eileen looked up suddenly. "You always did hate me, didn't you, Anne?"

Genuinely shocked, Anne denied it instantly. "How can you say such a thing, Eileen?"

"Because it's true, that's why. We've always been one of those cases like you read about. The little sister, always envious of the older sister who over-shadows her. She doesn't know it's hate, but it is. There was a case not long ago in the papers. A twelve-year-old girl took a gun and shot her sixteen-year-old sister, and afterwards, all she would say was that she'd always hated her sister and was glad she had killed her. Did you ever want to kill me, Anne?"

It was shocking to hear Eileen put that direct question in a flat, matter-of-fact voice. It was completely untrue, of course. Possibly there were such neurotic cases, but they had nothing to do with Anne's feeling about her sister. A touch of envy—Anne had always been willing to admit that much to herself. But it had never been too important, not enough to make her bitter or vindictive. And she had always been ready to offer Eileen a sincere and generous love. Only Eileen had never seemed to want it. Or to have the time to bother.

Anne reached for the pack of cigarettes on her bedside table. She rarely smoked, but she kept them there, just in case. She took one out, lit it, and handed it to Eileen. "You're letting your nerves get the best of you, honey. You're imagining stuff. If you really wanted me to play the devoted sister, nothing would please me more than to do it."

Still in that gentle, loving voice she continued: "That crazy stuff you just talked. It isn't worth replying to. Perhaps there've been times when I've wished I were a little more like you, because you're beautiful and you attract attention and love much more easily than I do. But that doesn't mean that I hate you, or resent you or ever have. And you said that Bob changed and started to hate you. I don't believe that, either."

"He hated some of the things about me. He said so." Eileen's sobbing had quieted, but there were still tears in her eyes.

"We started to have little quarrels. Don't ask me about what. Unimportant things. I'd have a crowd in during the afternoon and forget all about dinner. Bob would come home, hungry and tired, and get sore because nothing was ready to eat. He didn't like some of my friends. He didn't like being dragged out to dance, when he had planned to read or study. I said he couldn't expect me to poke around the house all day and not expect him to take me out and amuse me in the evening."

Eileen's short laugh was completely without humor. "It used to sound exactly like those funny strips. Well, one evening the going was more rugged than usual. I forget what I was so furious about. Anyway, I said I only wished I had never broken my engagement to Kenny Wilcox.

"Well," Eileen took a long, deep drag on the cigarette, "that did it. At first, Bob was all for calling everything quits. I apologized, tried to calm him down. He didn't calm. He told me straight to my face that I wasn't grown up enough to be married to anybody. He said that he doubted if I was in love with anybody—except myself. He said that I was just a spoiled, selfish, inconsiderate child. Finally he agreed not to insist on a divorce right away, but he refused to go on as we'd been doing. He said it was interfering with his work, slowly destroying him. He was determined to give up our apartment, put the furniture in storage. He was going to move to a hotel and I was to come home, forget that I had a husband, finish up my adolescence as he called it."

Eileen's small smile was grim. "You'd have thought he was telling a kid to go back and finish up school. That's exactly the way he treated me the last month or so—like a kid. And a not very bright one. Kenny Wilcox," Eileen explained, "was to be part of the program. Bob wanted me to see him, date him, find out exactly and for sure just how I felt about him. Bob said that he wanted no part of a wife who still imagined she was half in love with an old sweetheart."

Anne asked: "Didn't he know that Kenny and I were engaged?"

Eileen shook her head. "No. I didn't tell him. These quarrels started long before you wrote me about you and Kenny. When you did write—well, I just kept it to myself."

"I see." Anne was thoughtful. "Well," she said finally, "I'm sorry it was like that, Eileen. But maybe it will all straighten itself out. Possibly Bob did a very sensible thing. After you're separated for a time, you'll both know better how you feel about each other." She laughed. "I still don't see what all that has to do with your barging in here, accusing me of keeping Kenny away from your party."

Eileen said, smiling a trifle, completely honest for once: "Just the brat in me, I guess. Flying off the handle as usual, when I can't get my own way. Sometimes

I hate myself for being the way I am. When I stop and take a good look at myself, I do."

She added: "I guess that was the reason Bob got under my skin. Two or three times, he made me look at myself, and I didn't exactly like what I saw." Then, brightening, with the gay laugh that was more natural to her: "But let's face it. I am a spoiled brat. And the brat wants Kenny Wilcox to come to her party."

Already, Anne was beginning to wonder how much of Eileen's emotional outburst was the genuine article. Eileen had always been one for occasional attacks of heavy dramatics. Either way, Anne was sleepy. She needed her rest. She had to be up at six-thirty, and it was already after one. Ready to make any concession that would quiet Eileen, send her back to her own bed, Anne said: "Well, I'll tell you what, sis. I'll make it a point to see Kenny tomorrow. It may not do a bit of good. But I'll make it clear to him that I don't want him to skip the party on my account. Okay?"

CHAPTER 10

Alone, finally, with the room darkened, Anne found it impossible to sleep immediately after all. Her nerves refusing to relax? The tension refusing to release her? Or was it that for the very first time Alex Brooks presented a problem that called for a little serious thinking?

It was the first time that she had ever considered even the remote possibility that there might be a serious undertone to Alex's kidding remarks about marriage.

She did not really believe it now. Alex Brooks in love with her? Oh, impossible. Utterly impossible. And yet, as her mind ran back, she honestly wondered.

She thought of the times, not more than once or twice, when she had glanced up suddenly to catch his eyes fixed on her, and a certain look in them which at the time had surprised her vaguely. Warmth? Tenderness? Something even deeper, more urgent than tenderness?

Imagination, she told herself now. Sheer imagination. By mentioning Alex, Eileen had put the notion in her head. He thought of her as a friend, and nothing more.

Yet? Suddenly she recalled his eagerness to possess that painting of her. Which reminded her of Barney Fosdick, the artist, who had not as yet put in his appearance in Hillview. She must remember to ask Alex if he had heard any more from the man.

Go to sleep now, she told herself. You need your rest. You're supposed to be such a sensible girl, and this is a good time to remember it. Surely you have too much sense to indulge in any romantic moonings over Alex Brooks, of all people.

But the very thought of such a possibility had excited her emotionally. She could not resist asking herself exactly what she felt for Alex, or could feel, if she were to allow her emotions to run rampant.

The answer was very simply that she did not know.

She thought, lying there wide-eyed in the shadowy darkness, with the faintest slant of moonlight glimmering through one of the wide open windows, I think that I like Alex as well as any man I ever knew.

Yes. Even as well as she liked Kenny. There was, curiously, with Alex, a very strong sense of kindred spirits. They looked at so many questions in the same way. They enjoyed the same books. Both had a feeling for beautiful music, finding in it the expression of many of their own responses to life. Both had a sense of humor, invariably a strong bond between two people attracted to each other. It was, in a sense, the kind of attraction which often develops between the more quiet, introvert type of girl and an older man. But—

He was a lot older and there was no getting away from it. Anne couldn't recall that she had ever before thought of Alex in terms of his age. Yet the difference was there. Roughly, seventeen or eighteen years difference. Enough to make any serious difference, if she were to discover that he cared for her seriously, that she, by any wild chance, was a little in love with him? She wondered. Her reply to that question was a little grunt of complete exasperation with herself.

She sat up, thumped at her pillow, and turned over. Don't be a goop, she told herself with faint scorn. You know perfectly well that Alex Brooks isn't nursing any hopeless passion for you. And if you're ready to fancy yourself in love with him at the mere mention of such a thing, you're crazy. For one thing, you know perfectly well that you're not in love with him. Because if you were, you wouldn't be going into a cold sweat at the very thought of going to Kenny's office tomorrow. And why did you make that crazy promise to Eileen, anyway? Now go to sleep.

After that, she slept.

* * *

"What became of Barney Fosdick?" she asked Alex

the next morning. He was going over the morning mail at the moment. Anne had gone into his office to hunt a letter in his current files. "Did he change his mind about coming to Hillview?"

Alex grinned at her. "Not only do I have a capable secretary, but a psychic one as well. Here's a letter just came from Barney. He's driving over this afternoon, wants me to find a hotel room for him. He mentions you again. And that reminds me, how about bringing him over to your party tonight? Any objections?"

Anne grimaced. "It is no longer *my* party, chum. Do you think he'd want to come? After all, it will be mostly a young crowd, and he's an old man, also a famous and important man."

"And you don't think a famous, important artist is much the same as anybody else? You don't think an old fellow would enjoy looking in on a neat little gathering of the town's flaming youth? Anne, you're not a stupid girl. Yet there are times when you make unbelievably stupid remarks."

"Well," Anne objected stubbornly, "I don't think it's much of an idea."

"And I think it's an excellent idea. Furthermore, you want me to be on hand, so you say, and I can't very well leave the old fellow cooling his heels in a hotel lobby his first evening in town. Now can I?"

"Well."

"I'll tell you what. Suppose we leave it up to him. I'll ask Barney if he'd care to look in on a little gathering of the town's glamour girls. I'll explain that it will also be a chance for him to meet the girl who modeled for Girl In A Yellow Scarf and look her over in her native habitat. I'll tell him that he's invited to the party if he cares to come. Okay?"

They left it at that.

Anne offered to bet Alex a dime that the famous Barney Fosdick would elect to retire early and catch up on his beauty sleep. Then she promptly forgot the man.

It was such a rushed, busy morning that she forgot a lot of other things. For one, that she had planned to steal an hour to run over to the beauty parlor and have her hair set. When evening came, she really didn't want to look like something the cat had dragged in. She couldn't hope to compete with Eileen's glamour, the daring flame-colored dress, but, if only as a matter of pride, she shouldn't neglect her own appearance completely. She still hadn't decided what she would wear. She had a white evening dress (only a little over a year old) which would probably look as well as anything. However, she really had counted on doing something about her hair. But there was simply no time.

She was vaguely aware that Alex had gone out to lunch. Then—it came as a shock when she saw him returning—she looked at her watch and saw that it was getting close to two o'clock. "You going in for one of these starvation diets?" Alex asked. He made her stop in the middle of what she was doing. "Go eat," he ordered, and went on into his own office.

Anne took her bag out of the top drawer. Then, remembering Kenny and her promise to Eileen, she picked up the phone. Dr. Wilcox's office did not answer. Vaguely annoyed, she cradled the receiver. She should have phoned earlier. When it was possible, Kenny left the office early on Saturdays. Oh, well, she would stop into his office while she was out to lunch. It would only be a short walk out of her way, and the exercise would be good for her. If he was still not there, at least Eileen couldn't blame her for not trying to be as good as her word.

She left her desk, stepped into Alex's office to tell him that she might be a little late returning. She thought his look, as he glanced at her, was odd. Then he confessed without shame that he had heard her speaking to the operator to make sure that Dr. Wilcox did not answer.

"I was listening, deliberately. Even if I hadn't been, your voice carries."

"So what?" Anne said, half angry.

"So nothing at all. Except that, quite naturally, I'm jealous." His tone was bantering but his eyes were serious. "You told me you were off the guy and that he didn't object too vigorously. So a word of unwanted advice from another guy who doesn't want to see that unhappy look in your eyes. Don't go around begging for crumbs, honey. It's never paid off yet. Wait until he comes after you. You can take my word for it, kid, that sooner or later he will. But don't crawl, Anne. Don't go begging."

Since the advice was unwarranted, Anne didn't know whether to laugh in his face or scream with annoyance. She contented herself with saying smoothly: "Even the smartest lawyers make mistakes. If you think I'm crawling after Kenny, you're just plain silly."

Then, leaving it at that, she went to lunch.

Having little or no appetite, Anne settled for a drug store sandwich. And a malted milk which, as Nellie was forever reminding her, was so good and nourishing.

Eating took less than thirty minutes. Then she walked straight over to Kenny's office, refusing to let herself think what she was going to say when she got there.

She found him in. Very definitely he was in and probably had been when she phoned. Too occupied with other matters, no doubt, to bother answering the phone. For when she walked into his reception room, and then on into his small cubbyhole of an office, opening the door quietly, she found Kenny and Eileen. Since she walked in on them so unexpectedly, they did not have quite time enough to withdraw from each other's arms. Anne said, coolly enough: "Well, hello, darlings."

Kenny was the one to look thoroughly embarrassed. Anne saw the quick flush color his face, sensed the difficulty with which he managed to get out the completely inadequate words: "Well, hello, Anne. This is a surprise. I—we didn't expect you."

"No. I don't suppose you did." Anne laughed, amazed at her own coolness. Astonished that she seemed to feel so little of anything.

"Well, don't let it get you down. In fact as well as in fiction, ex-girl friends have a way of dropping in at the wrong moment. Oh, don't run off, Eileen, I'll not be here half a minute. By the time you've smoked a cigarette through, I'll be gone and," she managed a laugh, "you and Kenny can go back to catching up with all the time you've lost."

She turned back to Kenny who, for some reason, seemed to be growing more and more embarrassed by the second. He had looked for all the world like a kid caught stealing the jam. Anne dared to put a hand on his arm; both her eyes and her tone were completely friendly. Even more of a triumph, they seemed quite indifferent to the little scene she had witnessed.

She said: "Listen, Kenny, I came over to ask you to come to the party tonight. I want you to do it as a very special favor to me. Will you?"

Anne had him, she knew, in something of a spot. Eileen was sitting there, a small smile on her bright mouth, a look of quiet triumph in her shining eyes. With Eileen watching, listening, what could he say? None of the personal things that he might have brought up had he been talking with Anne alone.

He did try. "To tell you the truth, Anne, I've already made other arrangements."

"Then change them," Anne said swiftly. "Look, Kenny—and I don't at all mind Eileen hearing me say this—you mustn't let some quixotic notion about saving my feelings make you duck Eileen's party. It *is* her party, she's gone to a lot of trouble, and she wants all of her old friends there. I know she'll appreciate it if you come. Furthermore, let's face it, Kenny: This is a small town and you and I both live in it. We're going to have to go on seeing each other. After all, why shouldn't we? We were engaged for a little while and now we aren't. It's as simple as that, and certainly no reason for you to go around avoiding places where you might run into me as if I were a dose of poison."

Kenny looked perfectly miserable. "You know it isn't like that, Anne. You know that—"

Anne's laugh rang, gayer even than before. "Well, then, if it isn't like that, don't act like that. Like I said, we're bound to meet occasionally, and the sooner we learn to take it in stride the better. Tonight seems as good a time as any to get started. Please come, Kenny. Do it to please me. Won't you?"

Kenny, recovering from his embarrassment, was looking at her steadily. For a moment, he might have forgotten that Eileen was in the room, sitting not three feet from where he and Anne stood, facing each other. She had been all composure. Now, under his thoughtful, searching eyes, something in her seemed to melt. Not unlike an ice jam, suddenly giving way. Anne thought wildly, I've got to get out of here fast. Before I go completely to pieces.

What if he were to follow her as she went out, insist on talking with her alone? She both feared and hoped that he might. But in the end he did nothing of the sort. His eyes, so burning bright for a moment, seemed suddenly completely impersonal. And so was his quiet smile and the quality of his voice saying: "Very well, Anne. I promise you I'll show up. Can't have you saying I'm putting you in the poisonous category."

Then he left her bewildered, astonished, and a little angry by adding, as he half turned away from her: "By the way, I assume Alex Brooks will be on hand?"

"He will be," Anne admitted. "Only I can't think why you should assume any such thing."

Laughing, Eileen spoke up for the first time. "Now, Anne, darling. Don't try to play coy."

And Kenny added: "According to my spies who bring me up to date reports, the only time you and that guy aren't together is when you're on the way to meet each other."

Was Kenny jealous of Alex? To imagine it seemed neither logical nor sensible. But there had been a look in his eyes, a quality in his voice. And if he were?

The implications set her heart racing, but not for long.

A moment later she was down on the street, on the way back to her job and to Alex, and all she could think of was the picture of Kenny and Eileen clasped in each other's arms.

The bitterness of the hurt she felt, thinking of it, was frightening.

CHAPTER 11

The party, by Hillview standards, was a pretentious one. To one side of the wide center hall the two large, old-fashioned parlors had been thrown together, furniture moved out or close to the walls, the floors cleared for dancing. Electric bulbs gleamed like diamond sunbursts against the crystal ceiling chandeliers which Nellie steadfastly had refused to replace with more modern fixtures. "There's a certain elegance about crystal chandeliers," said Nellie. And why give up elegance for something both shoddy and ugly, simply to be in style?

For decorations, there were massed banks of autumn leaves making a tapestry of colors, reds and yellows and browns, and against them tall vases of chrysanthemums, yellow and bronze.

To the other side of the hall the dining-room table had been extended to its full length. The Chinese lace tablecloth which covered it was very fine, very rare, and had been one of Nellie's wedding presents. She had never allowed it to be used except on "very special occasions," never allowed it to be laundered except by hand. To-night was the first time she had brought it out since Eileen's wedding.

The floral centerpiece, deep red, hot-house roses against a mass of waxy, lush green leaves, had been Eileen's idea. She could, she had said, have thought up a flower arrangement with much more originality. But she had fancied the idea of the roses in combination with her flame-colored dress. Very effective, she had decided, when she brought the guests out to the dining room and they stood drinking a champagne toast.

Champagne Eileen had positively insisted upon, de-spite her mother's mild protest that people in Hillview simply did not give champagne parties. It was so easy to start unpleasant talk. "Let the natives talk," Eileen laughed. "A little champagne never hurt anybody and it puts life in a party."

Practically everyone in town who "was anybody" had been invited. Nellie had arranged to have refreshments served upstairs for the older crowd, her own special friends, two or three cousins who had been invited, and, of course, Aunt Molly and Uncle Ned. The younger guests included eight or ten officers from Fort Prendle. With the exception of the very skittish Colonel Andy Ritter, Eileen was sure that the "brass" would all show up. To the last minute, however, she seemed concerned about the tall, blond, and very elusive Texan.

According to Eileen, every gal in town who had met this Ritter character had made a play for him with no luck at all. He asked for no dates, had refused all invitations. It would be, Eileen admitted frankly, quite a feather in her cap if the lad came to her party. And she was simply going to die if he didn't show.

It was nearly seven o'clock when Anne came home that evening. Eileen called from her room as Anne went upstairs: "Well, it's a wonder you bothered to come home at all. I suppose it never occurred to you that there has to be some last minute getting ready for a brawl like this and that you could have helped."

Eileen's heavy sarcasm wasn't lost on Anne. She found it both amusing and exasperating. She might very well have retorted: "I suppose it never occurs to you that this was to have been my own engagement party and that, as of now, it's simply an unpleasant reminder of how my own pretty little dreams blew up in my face."

She stopped at the door of Eileen's room.

The stunning flame dress was laid out on the bed. Eileen, in a pretty negligee, was seated in front of her dressing table mirror, her soft hands touching crystal jars and bottles. Anne bit back the bitter words which sprang to her lips, contented herself with a faint smile, and said: "Sorry if I seem to have let you down, sis. But after all, I do have a job and it's been a terrific day.

Since you're the star of this show tonight, I thought I might just as well let you handle the stage setting and lighting effects, too."

Through the mirror, she saw Eileen's surprisingly hostile glance. Last night, for a few minutes, they had approached something like sisterly closeness, but Eileen seemed to have forgotten that little outburst, the confidences she had made.

She might also have forgotten that Anne had walked in and found her and Kenny making love. At any rate, she made no mention of it. And Anne had no intention of bringing it up. "Well, I guess I'd better run along and fix up a little," Anne said.

"What are you planning on wearing, dear?" Eileen's tone was caustic, behind the simulated sweetness. "Maybe those blue jeans you wear to work in the garden?"

Anne laughed. "Was that necessary? How often must I remind you, Eileen, this is your party. Those officers who are coming here are your little pals, not mine. Most of the town crowd are kids who were much closer friends of yours than mine. I'm sorry if I haven't shown much interest or had the time to do very much to help with the arrangements. But I don't see why you should make nasty cracks or try to make an issue of it. So I didn't get a new dress, and I didn't have time to get my hair set. What does it matter?"

"Well, I don't like your attitude," Eileen retorted.

"That's what matters. It's just more of the same way you've been acting right along." Her tone was that of a petulant, peevish child who was not receiving the attention she wanted. "You resent my coming home, that's what it amounts to. You resent everything I do. You resent my giving this party."

There were times, Anne decided, when you might just as well say exactly what you were thinking. With a frowning glance in the direction of Eileen's exquisitely soft, bared shoulders, she let her have it. "Okay. I do resent this party. Everything about it makes me bitter and angry and sick to my stomach. And you might just as well know it. My engagement to Kenny was to have been announced at this party, and if you expect me to forget that, you're crazy. Neither can you expect me to go all to pieces with gratitude over the way you coaxed me to use my influence to get Kenny to come tonight and then I walk in on you and Kenny making love. I resent all of it, and if you want to make anything of it, go right ahead. I'll come downstairs tonight and try to act pretty with all the boys and girls. But you needn't expect me to like it, because I don't. And if it weren't that it might look funny and cause talk, I wouldn't show my face."

Then Anne stalked across the hall to her room, banging the door behind her.

She stood for a moment, catching her breath, regretting that she'd lost control of herself. Oh, well. Then her glance went longingly to the bed. Nothing she wanted more than to throw herself down, relax for twenty minutes or so. But if she did, it would delay her dressing that much longer.

As she was stripping off her clothes, Nellie, pretty and surprisingly youthful-appearing in gray taffeta, came into the room. She, too, was reproachful. "Anne, I don't think you're treating Eileen very nicely. You know how excited she is over this party. The least you could do is show a little interest."

"And if I haven't any interest?" Anne said. Why couldn't her mother, at least, understand that tonight was a kind of exquisite torture for her? She had a wild impulse to run out of the room, down the stairs and out of the house, screaming.

No one gives a thought to my feelings, she thought bitterly. No one cares. Or, with grim amusement, maybe she wasn't supposed to have feelings, give way to temperamental outbursts. Possibly such emotional luxuries should be reserved for the beauty of the family. The birthright of Eileen, the prima donna.

Anne caught herself up sharply.

She realized that she was letting her nerves get the best of her. Because she was so beastly tired? Or because the stabbing hurt of seeing Kenny and Eileen together had gone deeper than she wanted to admit, even to herself? Get yourself together, honey, she said aloud. You're a big girl now, so stop behaving like a disgruntled baby.

After a hot and then a cold shower, a brisk rubdown with a heavy towel, she felt better.

She hunted through her closet and found a dress she had almost forgotten that she had. It was two years old, not in the latest style. But the lines were good; the neck, square cut, and the tiny puffed sleeves had always looked charming on her. The sapphire blue shade went beautifully with the deeper blue of her eyes. She thought whimsically that it was the kind of dress Alex would probably like on her. She decided to put it on.

She was regretful again that she hadn't had time to do anything about having her hair set. Fortunately, it had a natural wave. She took out the pins, brushed it for a minute or so, then repinned it in the somewhat severe style which she had decided looked as well on her as any other, and was less bother.

By the time Anne got downstairs, the three piece colored orchestra was tuning up, the guests arriving. Eileen in her sophisticated dress, very low in the back, was darting about like a living flame, laughing, kissing everyone, first the center of one little group and then of another.

Anne stood for a moment at the foot of the stairway, watching her vivid sister. How she loves this sort of thing, Anne thought, knowing that she was a little envious—not so much of Eileen's sparkle and radiance as of the youthful, never-dying enthusiasm which made her thrill and respond as she did to the excitement of a party. Anne admitted to herself ruefully, I guess I was born a little old woman. "I don't believe I've ever had the pleasure of meeting you. My name is Ritter. Andy Ritter."

Startled, Anne looked up, and met the quietly smiling blue eyes of the very good-looking young officer who had materialized, as if by magic, beside her. She smiled back at him. "I'm Eileen's sister, and you're Colonel Ritter." He was, as Eileen had reported, extremely good-looking. And he loathes parties. Anne guessed that about the man, before he admitted it in so many words. "I hail from the Texas cow country. I know how to handle a herd of balking steers, but darned if I know how to handle myself on a dance floor. And all these sophisticated glamour girls scare me stiff. I feel as if they're laughing at me." He added: "I can tell you this because you seem different somehow. You seem more the quiet type."

Anne laughed. "Those gals are all in love with you, Colonel. Didn't you know?" The remark seemed to fill him with mild, half whimsical terror. "But don't let it throw you," Anne added soothingly. "Our Hillview girls fall in love with surprising ease. Just an old Virginia custom. They fall out of love just as easily. And I am the quiet type."

"So am I," said Andy Ritter, his voice hearty, his eyes still holding that quiet smile. "So what do you say we find some secluded corner and start brushing up on the things we don't know about each other?"

Anne looked doubtful. "But you just came in, didn't you? There are so many you haven't met."

His glance was pleading. "Must I? Honest, Anne, have pity on me. I don't want to be rude, but if you could only know how I dread being marched around a drawing room and introduced to strange people. I can get acquainted with them on my own okay, but to make little bows and chirp little nothings—"

Anne laughed, genuinely liking him. It wasn't any pose, or a line he was handing her. He really was the shy type, when it came to making the expected social gestures. She caught his hand. "Come along with me, Colonel. Obviously, we're two of a kind. Eileen has the center of the stage, so no one expects much of me. I'll never be missed. You and I will go back to the study. It's the coziest room in the house. Also, it's the one room in the house that doesn't know there's a party on. The chairs are comfortable, the lights are restful, it's a nice room to get acquainted in."

"Sounds grand," said the colonel, following her.

It was in the study, a smallish room tucked away at

the far side of the dining room, that Eileen found them thirty minutes later.

Eileen was looking daggers. Eileen's angry eyes implied that she could cheerfully slit Anne's throat, giving the lie to the bright, forced smile on her lips. "Anne, dear, how dreadfully selfish of you, appropriating the colonel like this. Andy Ritter, you rate a sound scolding. I've been looking for you everywhere. I've been dying, simply dying to dance with you. But no you."

"I'm a rotten dancer," Andy stated flatly.

Eileen laughed gaily. "A flimsy excuse. And no matter. I mean to dance with you." Then, to Anne: "Alex Brooks is asking for you. He just arrived. He has someone with him. Some old freak who looks like Santa Claus. If you don't mind my suggesting it, Anne, I hope you'll get rid of this old party as soon as possible. I can't think where Alex picked up such a queer-looking character, or why he should have brought him to my party."

Anne darted to her feet. "Freak! Don't show your ignorance, Eileen," her voice sharper than she had intended. "It's probably Barney Fosdick."

"And who might Barney Fosdick be?" inquired Eileen with an air of supreme indifference. "Frankly, he strikes me as an old bum who could use both a shave and a fresh shirt."

Andy Ritter, surprisingly, appeared both amused and irritated by such ignorance. "My dear girl," he informed

Eileen, whose face colored with angry embarrassment, as she realized she had made a fool of herself, "if it's the Barney Fosdick I think it is, he can afford the eccentricity of a beard if he likes. He's a famous artist and one of the finest this country has ever produced."

"Oh," Eileen said. Then, hopefully: "Well, I don't think it can be the same man. After all, why would a famous artist be in such a dither to meet our little Anne?"

CHAPTER 12

At first glance, Barney Fosdick appeared to be what the world of conventional folks invariably refers to as "a character." A heavy white beard all but concealed the fine, sensitive structure of his face. Merry blue eyes which had learned, a long time ago, that it was as simple to laugh over the foibles of a confused, bewildered world as to cry, and more pleasant. His way of dressing, as Eileen had suggested, was unusual—judged by conventional standards. Although she had been wrong about the shirt. Tan, similar to the type worn by army men, it was immaculately clean, an expensive make. The sleeves, to be sure, flaunted two or three large patches over presumably worn spots. But these, like the riding breeches, the polished leather boots, were a kind of Barney Fosdick trademark. A form of self-advertisement. Or, more accurately, his manner of dressing (quaint, outlandish, picturesque, according to the viewpoint) had, in its inception, grown out of a determination to attract attention to himself.

Later, when there was no further need to "advertise," he decided that the costume was a very comfortable one, and it did not trouble him to be considered odd. Or an exhibitionist. Or an old poser. Which, as he sometimes related to his intimates, was exactly what he had been, some thirty odd years earlier. And no doubt still was. Only these days, shocking people was one of his forms of amusement. In the earlier days, when he was a mere youth, he had lived in a dismal, garret kind of Greenwich Village room. Not caring too much that his food was scant, the seat of his trousers worn through, he was, nevertheless, resentful, bitter, discouraged, because he knew that the paintings he was doing were good, yet he was unable to achieve recognition of any sort or to make a dime off of his work. He was all but ready to give up.

Then a practical-minded man had advised him: "My boy, that yarn about the mouse-trap and the world beating a path to your door—take it with a grain of salt. First you've got to make the world know where the mouse-trap is to be found."

Shortly thereafter, Barney was to be found on a Village sidewalk, complete with beard, New York's conception (mostly erroneous) of a rugged cowboy costume, and, of course, his easel. For four bits he would do a sketch of anyone who came along. That was the way he made his first money from his art. His sketches were skillful and, much later, worth a great deal of money. But it was his curious getup, not his talent which was close to genius, which attracted his first customers.

When Anne, a little diffident, walked toward the front hall, she heard Barney's booming laugh before she saw the man. Then Alex caught sight of her, smiled and caught her arm. "You look lovely tonight," he whispered, a bit of flattery which Anne was quick to deny. "I do not. I look a mess. Feel like one, too."

Then Barney Fosdick turned. Already he was the center of a group of girls. He had always had quite a way with women, had two ex-wives, famous beauties, and several love affairs with well-known actresses, to prove it. Even now (and he was well past sixty) women had a way of falling in love with him. A Hollywood star had once explained it for the press: "Barney understands women better than they understand themselves." Which, she had added, was probably the secret of all the Don Juans the world had ever known.

The most insidious, most irresistible gift of all. To look into a woman's eyes and let her see the reflection of herself in his own eyes. With that one little knack, a man could go far with women. Even when he was ninety. Barney walked up to Anne. He caught her hands, his bright and surprisingly blue eyes looked her up and down. "Well," he said finally, and his voice boomed so that everyone in the house could hear every word he uttered, "this is the little girl I traveled all the way from New York to have a look at. And it was worth it."

Tongue-tied with embarrassment, with the knowledge that everyone was watching her, Anne couldn't think of a single solitary word to say. She felt the swift color flood her cheeks; then, more self-conscious than ever, she heard Barney chuckling. "Why, you're blushing, by golly. Now I take that as the biggest form of flattery. See what I told you, Alex? I'm not such an old dodo, after all. As long as I can still get a blush out of a pretty girl, what am I worrying about?"

Anne's tension eased then, as Eileen reappeared, had to be introduced. Barney said, amused: "This girl your sister, Anne? I'd never know it. Hello, Eileen. You took me for some old tramp when Alex walked me in, didn't you?" His hearty laugh boomed. "Now, now, don't try to deny it." He wagged a finger at her. "Your face was a dead giveaway. Don't worry about it, girl. No offense if you did mistake me for an old bum. Some of my best friends are bums. Still can't believe that you two girls are sisters, however."

Anne had recovered her composure. She said, smiling: "We don't look a bit alike, do we? Eileen is the beauty of the family, while I—"

"While you what?" The old man was suddenly scowling, a fierce scowl.

"Well, I'm the plain one," Anne said.

"Nonsense. Utter nonsense. Nothing plain about you. Know why I was so struck with that painting of you? Know why I wanted to meet you? Because you're the spit and image of my first sweetheart. I was eleven at the time and she——" He named an actress of the gay nineties era, one of the greatest of them all. "You look more like Lily," Barney said, "than Lily looked like herself. And I ought to know. Used to save up every nickel I could scrape together. When I got enough of them, I'd buy me a matinee gallery seat. Then for three enchanted hours I'd sit and feast my eyes on my Great Love. She seemed the most beautiful thing on earth to me. Still does, although she's been dead for thirty years. Not the more obvious kind of beauty, of course. Not the kind that can be bought over a drug store counter and walks up and knocks a man in the eye. Oh, no, nothing like that. Some people have even gone so far as to call Lily a plain woman. They said it was only when she was acting, when she gave out all the warmth and wealth of her personality, that her real loveliness shone out. And perhaps they were partly right. Perhaps Lily's fundamental loveliness, her great beauty, was an inner spiritual quality, something she could turn on or off as she chose. But she was a great actress. When men loved her—and a great many men did—it was a kind of worship that they gave her. I doubt if any man who loved Lily ever forgot her or ever found anyone like her again. And to me she was a great beauty."

His eyes came back to Anne, softening wonderfully as he studied her. He patted her cheek, smiling. "I still say you're the image of Lily. Looking at you takes me right back. So did that painting Julian Lowry did of you. Got it hanging where I can look at it, every morning first thing when I wake up. Take it with me everywhere I go." He chuckled. "Your sweetheart here, Alex, has been trying to get me to part with it. Not a chance. Don't mean to part with it as long as I'm alive and kicking. My friend Alex has the original; little enough favor to let an old fellow like myself have the picture."

Kenny walked in just in time to catch these last words. Anne, meeting his eyes as he paused in the hallway, flushed crimson. "Alex isn't my sweetheart, Mr. Fosdick."

Alex spoke up, laughing. "No, Barney, get it straight. Alex is just the guy who proposes every hour on the hour. But as yet, no luck."

After that, it was Anne's evening.

She would always suspect that Alex had put the artist up to his little act which, act or no act, succeeded in centering attenton upon herself, although Alex denied solemnly that he had done any such thing.

The guests, most of them carefree youngsters who knew nothing of art or artists, were all agog when they discovered that Barney Fosdick was an outstanding artist, according to some a genius. This, in turn, caused them to consider Anne with new eyes. Shy, plain little Anne Veigh, whom Barney Fosdick had come all the way from New York to look at. They kept looking at her, watching her, and to their surprise Anne suddenly and actually did seem to be blooming like a rose.

She was laughing, gay, giving out with charm. "Why, what's happened to Anne?" they whispered. "I've never seen her like this before. She seems so vital."

And so she did.

Slowly, under Barney's skillful touch, and he scarcely left her side the rest of the evening, Anne seemed to come out of her shell.

He whispered nonsense to her and her eyes sparkled with laughter.

He kept repeating how she reminded him of that great actress of his youth, and Anne, not believing a word of it, was nonetheless flattered. After all, it *could* be true. And the very possibility gave her a heightened sense of her own charm.

Barney said, when Kenny came up to them: "And who is this gloomy-looking young man? He looks to me like the victim of a love affair that was going none too well. Have you been cruel to him, young lady? Turned down his love? Set him adrift on a loveless ocean?"

Anne retorted gaily: "This is Kenny Wilcox, Mr.

Fosdick, and you guessed it right, only in reverse. He's turned me down."

Barney shook his head. "It doesn't seem possible. He doesn't look such a fool. Young man, perhaps what you need is a metabolism test."

Anne giggled: "But he's a doctor, Mr. Fosdick."

"So that proves what?" The artist gave her one of his more ferocious scowls. "I happen to have a very low opinion of the average doctor, and as a very special favor, my dear, would you kindly refrain from addressing me as Mr. Fosdick? Makes me feel as old as Methuselah."

Kenny, catching her in the hall for a moment, tried to make her go outside with him and seemed both hurt and angry when she refused. "I want to talk with you, Anne. I want to explain about what happened at my office today."

Aloof, very independent in her new-found self-assurance, Anne inquired coldly: "You mean about you and Eileen? I don't think there's anything to explain, Kenny. I really don't."

"Oh, don't be like that, Anne. Honey, baby, please—" She had never seen him so agitated, and there seemed to be a very real torment in his eyes. He caught her in his arms, but she was away from him instantly, swift anger in her eyes. "I don't like that, Kenny. I don't like it a little bit. Eileen is the one you want and I don't doubt you can have her if you try real hard. But let me alone."

"And if I were to tell you that I don't want Eileen?"

She stared back at him, feeling weak for a moment, saying over his words to herself. Words that were offering her a miracle? But her heart, having skipped a beat or two, resumed its quiet, steady pace. After all, she had seen what she had seen—Kenny's head bent to Eileen's flushed, beautiful face; Eileen's shining, soft eyes; Kenny's arms holding her in love. . . . "Who do you think you're kidding?" she said coldly. She turned her back on him and walked swiftly back to where Barney and Alex were standing together.

And it was then that Barney said to her: "Anne, honey, I want to see you just as you were in that painting. Your hair loosened, the yellow scarf around your throat. Please?"

Anne laughed, hesitated. "The scarf was just an old thing. I haven't an idea where it is. Is it important?"

"To me, yes." The old man was very serious. "I am very anxious to have that picture of you, in the flesh, to carry with me in my mind. If it isn't too much trouble, honey."

Alex offered, laughing: "If you can't find the scarf, I'll dash out and buy you half a dozen new ones."

She found the scarf, folded and stacked with her best handkerchiefs in the satin case in a bureau drawer. Then, loosening her hair, Anne looked at herself in the mirror, laughing a little. She wasn't sure that she had the nerve to go downstairs with her hair spraying over her shoulders. She was afraid that she would look silly. . . . She thought suddenly, "That's been one of my troubles. I've always been so afraid of looking silly. Only what I've really meant was that I was afraid of attracting attention to myself. Now, tonight, someone else had attracted attention to her, deliberately tossed her into the limelight, and look how well it was turning out. Already she felt a curious assurance she had never known before. Already she felt a kind of beauty about herself. Still studying her reflection, it seemed to her that she looked nearer to beautiful than she ever had before.

Dimly, very dimly, she sensed what the explanation was. Barney Fosdick had made her feel important.

No one had ever done that for her before.

Her mother, Eileen, even many of her friends—to all of them she had always been plain, sensible little Anne. The one who would never win any beauty prizes. The one who need not expect particularly exciting things to happen to her because she simply was not the type to whom such things did happen. Anne—a swell girl and very capable and dependable. Anne—of no importance at all. A nice enough girl, however. The salt of the earth, so to speak. But no glamour girl. This had been impressed upon her straight down the years, and so it had become the version of herself which Anne had accepted.

Barney Fosdick, a funny old character with a touch of artistic genius and a keen insight into human nature, had lifted her right out of it. He had compared her to one of the loveliest and most gifted actresses who had ever appeared on the American stage. With a few clever words he had made her old friends stare at her and see a loveliness in her that had never occurred to them before.

He had, with a phrase quickly turned at the right moment, set Kenny to worrying. Oh, yes, there had been a very real worry in Kenny's eyes. Anne was sure of it. Kenny was beginning to wonder, she thought wryly, if he was giving up a more precious jewel than he had realized.

Barney Fosdick had, in short, made her feel important and lovely. Whether it was all true or not did not matter. He had given her the feeling that she possessed a charm, a loveliness, quite unknown to herself. And the feeling seemed to have kindled a light inside her.

Her own eyes, looking back at her from the mirror, held a sparkling brilliance she had never noticed in them before. Her sweetly curved lips wore a more radiant smile. She touched her fingertips to her cheeks, felt their petal smoothness. She said softly: "I've always been such a washout and I do believe it's half my own fault."

She picked up the yellow scarf then, wound it carelessly around her throat. After that she went downstairs.

CHAPTER 13

In the morning Eileen, pleading a violent headache, did not come down to breakfast. And when she appeared around noon, wanting only black coffee, she insisted that she felt perfectly awful. When Nellie suggested sympathetically: "Too much party, dear?" Eileen retorted shortly: "Oh, don't mention that miserable affair. I was never so bored."

Anne, coming into the kitchen to get a drink of water, smiled to herself.

She knew what the trouble was. All of those officers wanting dates with Anne. Andy Ritter making an obvious play for her, inviting her to the officers' club next Saturday night and refusing to take no for an answer.

And Barney Fosdick, when Anne appeared in the yellow scarf with her hair cascading like pale yellow silk, enthusing over the artistic effect. Barney proclaiming that she was a real artist's beauty. Barney making them all drink a champagne toast to The Girl In The Yellow Scarf.

Then, Alex Brooks, after a few too many glasses of champagne, announcing in his best style that Anne was the gal he intended to marry.

"Haven't got the lady's okay as yet," Alex grinned. "But just give me time. The lad who always gets his woman, that's me. Only our Anne is the first little lovely I've happened to want in a big way." Then, turning to Anne who stood near him, putting his arm lightly around her: "How's about giving me a break, honey? Say the word right now and dash the hopes of every other gal in the room."

Laughing, "Oh, Alex, you idiot you. Don't you dare take another drop of that champagne." Anne had pushed him away from her. It was a few minutes before she noticed that Kenny was gone, very abruptly, without saying good-night to anyone.

It had all added up to little Anne becoming suddenly and unexpectedly the belle of the ball. And Eileen was fit to be tied, because she was unused to having the limelight deflected away from her.

She said now, crossly, over the coffee which she complained was too hot: "That silly old man. He struck me as half-witted. If he was a sample of a great artist, then deliver me from any more of the same. I say he's cracked."

"Because he said that I was attractive?" Anne inquired sweetly.

Eileen's eyes came up, looking her over, and Anne was amazed at the spiteful look in them. She's so young, Anne thought pityingly. Emotionally, Eileen was like a selfish child of about seven who simply could not endure seeing another child have a beautiful doll to play with. Eileen said contemptuously: "Obviously, the old fool has a case on you. Lots of silly old men are like that. Go about imagining they're still young—falling in love with young girls. I don't see how you could stomach his silly talk, Anne. I thought you had too much sense. He certainly wouldn't be my cup of tea."

Then, with a disdainful shrug: "Of course, I know some girls are like that. Anything to have a man make a fuss over them, even if he has one foot in the grave. But I wouldn't have expected it of you. I really wouldn't have."

Anne walked over to the table and looked her sister right in the eye. She had never come so close to positive dislike. "Look, Eileen, I know the party didn't go to suit you. One or two people paid a little attention to me for a change, and that you can't stand. Well, you'd better learn to stand it. If you think the whole world is going to spoil you and palaver over you for the rest of your days, you're in for some unpleasant surprises. Bob got wise to you and sent you packing. Sooner or later there will be others who will do the same thing if you don't get wise to yourself. As for me, I'm sick and tired of sitting on the sidelines, watching you play leading lady. And if you make any more ugly, insulting insinuations, like that one you just made about Barney Fosdick, I'm getting out of this house. And I'll stay out, as long as you're in it."

Nellie, who was fussing with something on the stove, said mildly: "Now, girls, don't get to quarreling. Really, Anne. You shouldn't talk that way to Eileen. You know the poor child is suffering with a headache."

"Headache, my eye! The 'poor child' is suffering from a hangover from a party where she lost hold of the ball and never got it back. But I wouldn't expect you to see that, Mother. Anything that Eileen says or does is right and anything I say is wrong. It's always been that way in this house. Just because I've always stood for it doesn't mean that I'm not good and sick and fed up with it. But when Eileen starts making nasty digs about a wonderful, gifted man like Barney Fosdick, when she tells me to my face that I'm man-crazy—"

"Well, you are," Eileen retorted. "You've never got much attention from men, and once you do get a little flattery it goes straight to your head. I wasn't going to tell you this, but now I think I might as well say it. You made a perfect little fool of yourself last night. If you want to know, I was actually ashamed of you. I don't think there's anything more sickening than one of these shy, plain little models who suddenly fancies herself as the life of the party and starts to make a show of herself. And that's what you did. I'm very sorry to have to tell you, Anne. You made a regular spectacle of yourself." And Eileen laughed, for the first time that morning.

Anne stared back at her sister, afraid to speak for fear she'd say ugly, unforgivable things that she'd regret. Then she glanced at her mother who, to make matters worse, was saying: "Well, Anne dear, there may be something in what Eileen is saying. Of course I wasn't downstairs. I don't know exactly what went on. But you seem to have been a little gay. Loosening your hair, putting on that scarf, letting that old man pose you with those roses from the centerpiece. Eileen went to so much trouble with that decoration I can't blame her for not liking having it all torn to pieces. And my lovely tablecloth spoiled with all that water spilled over it. You're scarcely the type, dear, to let yourself go the way you seem to have done. I think you probably forgot yourself just a little."

Anne didn't take her eyes off her mother while she was talking. When she had finished, Anne didn't say a word. She simply stood for a moment, staring at nothing at all.

Then, without a word, she left the kitchen and went up to her room. She was scarcely aware of what she was doing as she got two bags out of her closet and started to pack.

"Now, Anne, I want you to stop this nonsense. The very idea. Threatening to leave home because Eileen has a headache and said things she didn't mean." Nellie came in, both troubled and irritated.

Threat was scarcely the word. Anne folded a night-gown, her lounging robe, tucked in a pair of bedroom slippers. "This is something I should have done long ago, Mother." Eileen, making her sore, had simply helped her to muster up a little courage she had long needed. "I've often thought I'd be happier if I could get away from home for a while, live my own life." And, of course, not have the reminder of Eileen's superior charms crammed down her throat every time she moved or turned.

"I've accused Eileen of not being grown up. Well," Anne said quietly, "in a sense, I'm not grown up either. If I were, I wouldn't be scared of so many things. I'm scared of meeting people. If anything nice happens to me, I'm scared that it won't last. I was so scared that Eileen would take Kenny away from me when she came home that I turned him loose without waiting to see what happened. I was too scared to wait, too scared to put up a fight."

Her smile was rueful. "I'm practically scared of my own shadow, Mother. I wouldn't be if I were grown up."

And maybe if she got away from the nest, tried meeting life and people completely on her own, she would grow up, she thought.

"Right this minute," Anne confessed, "I'm scared at the thought of what I'm doing." But she was going to.

Such talk. Nellie tried ridicule, then argument. She had always felt that a girl's place, until she married, was in her own home with her mother. She could not get used to the modern way: a girl picking up and walking out when she felt like it. She did not want to get used to it. All this loose talk about there being more chance for "self-development" when a girl was on her own was simply high-sounding phrases. What it really came to was that Anne wanted to be free of all restraint and discipline, a chance to "cut loose," said Nellie, with such vigorous emphasis that Anne had to laugh.

"Now, Mother, don't talk nonsense." The last thing Anne could be ashamed of, surely, was any tendency to "cut loose."

And if it were true. Another quiet chuckle. "I suspect that a little cutting loose would do me good." In a small southern town where the accepted behavior for an unmarried girl was still cut to a fairly old-fashioned pattern. Had Anne ever caused a word of criticism? She rarely smoked, never was seen in cocktail bars or road houses. And certainly no one could accuse her of light affairs with men, since she wasn't the type who seemed to attract that sort of thing.

"When you come right down to it, Mother, I'm next thing to a prig."

Then she went around the bed to Nellie, who was sobbing softly. A last resort? Sorrowful tears, the last refuge of the possessive mother who could not bear to see her young spreading their wings to leave the nest?

Anne sat down beside her. "Mother, please. The last thing I want to do is hurt you. Look at it this way. I haven't been too happy. I've missed a lot of the fun and thrills that a lot of girls take as their rightful due and I truly think that it's because I'm much too shy." She smiled. "I've had a kind of Eileen complex. If I live by myself for a while, make a few ventures on my own, I think it will do me good. Anyway, I have the right to try. And I promise you I won't do it in such a way as to cause talk. Aunt Molly has an extra bedroom. I'm sure she'll let me stay with them for a while. Then I may decide to leave town, try a city."

Nellie looked up, scandalized. "Where in the world would you go? What would you do?"

"I haven't an idea, Mother. I'm not even sure that I will do anything of the sort. I merely mentioned the possibility. I've often thought that I'd like to go away for a while, just for the experience."

Then her face hardened as she heard her mother saying: "I won't permit it, Anne. You simply cannot leave home like this because it's going to hurt Eileen. The dear girl will feel that she's driven you out."

Anne stood up, and her voice came cool, utterly devoid of feeling. "I'm sorry, Mother. But at the moment I'm simply not in the mood to worry about Eileen's feelings."

Aunt Molly was delighted to see her, thrilled at the prospect of having Anne, her favorite, for an indefinite visit. Uncle Ned, too. "Make yourself right at home, Anne. Stay as long as you like. Good for Molly and me to have a little youth around the place. Only one thing I won't stand for. Don't let me catch you snitching my cigars. Sensible thing you're doing, Anne, cutting loose from Nellie's apron strings. Want to know a secret, girl? Nellie had a reason you never caught onto for keeping you in the background. It wasn't only because her precious Eileen was such a knockout, she thinks. There was more to it than that. Nellie didn't want you to get a lot of attention and marry in a hurry, because then she'd be completely alone. She couldn't bear that idea. If she could have turned you into an old maid, it would have been her protection against a lonely old age. I ain't saying she even knew she had any such mean idea. Lot of mothers are like that. Selfish, without ever knowing they're selfish. Waste a girl's youth and call it unselfish mother love. Worst of it is, they sure enough believe they're unselfish. Derned if they don't."

It was a curious idea, one that had never occurred to Anne before. Aunt Molly, however, promptly discouraged any further such analytical discussions. "Nellie means all right," she observed. "She just doesn't think. Anne has come to us, and I'm glad. I think every girl should get away from home. It's the best way in the world to develop self-reliance. You're welcome to stay here as long as you like, honey. But if you decide to branch out a bit more, go to some city, Uncle Ned and I will help you in any way we can. You're the nearest thing to a daughter of our own we've ever had. We love you very much. Always remember that. Now. This room is yours. We've grown lazy, don't get up some mornings until after nine. So maybe you'd rather get your own breakfasts. We have dinner at six-thirty. There'll always be an extra plate for you. If you're late, or have other dinner arrangements, don't worry about it. Feel free to come and go as you like."

Aunt Molly went over and put her arms around Anne. Not a demonstrative woman, Anne knew that this was an extraordinary show of affection for her to make. Anne was even more deeply touched, found her eyes swimming, when Aunt Molly said softly: "We love you very much, child. We're happy to have you with us."

Before she had finished unpacking her things, getting them arranged in the closet, she was called to the phone.

Alex Brooks. "I called your house. Your ma said you'd gone over to your aunt's for a few days' visit."

Anne told him, laughing: "That's Mother's always-the-well-bred-southern-lady version. Actually, there was a battle royal on the home front this morning, so little Anne whipped together a few scraps of courage and moved out. According to sister Eileen, I tried to be the life of the party last night and made myself ridiculous. Could be she was right. How would I know since I'm the type who gets drunk on a few words of flattery? Did I act silly, Alex?"

The words were self-revealing. She had worried, vaguely, that there might have been truth to what Eileen said. Alex said, downright angry: "It would be a real pleasure to tell that bratty sister of yours where to get off. A walking edition of the green-eyed monster when she isn't the center of attention." He laughed. "Tell Eileen to go take a jump in a nice, deep lake. Do her good. You were lovely, Anne, and if you don't want to take my word for it, take it up with our expert on charming ladies. Barney wants us—you and me—to have dinner in his room at the hotel. I'll pick you up around six o'clock. Okay?"

Then he added unexpectedly: "I ran into your boy friend this morning. He and I picked the same moment to drop into the drug store for a cup of coffee. Kenny looked to me like a man who had spent a bad night nursing his battered heart. You didn't have much time for him last night, and in my humble judgment, he took it hard."

Anne pretended a deep sigh. "Ah, Alex, what would I do without you? Always ready with a word of cheer and comfort, and even though I know it isn't true, it sounds good."

He said, astonished: "Anne, do you mean to tell me you don't realize that Kenny Wilcox is sick in love with you? Did you happen to notice his eyes watching you last night? Well, I did. However—" He laughed. "What am I saying! Why should I plead another man's cause when I'm the fellow who wants to marry you?"

Then, at her quick. skeptical laugh, he seemed actually angry. His words fairly sizzled over the wire. "So help me, Anne Veigh, you're either the dumbest proposition I've ever come across or else you're putting on an act. And I know that you're not dumb. If you don't understand by this time that I'm serious about wanting to marry you, then you ought to go somewhere and have your head examined."

With that he hung up, and Anne stood for a moment, her eyes large and startled, staring at the phone as if it were a *live* thing. He *means* it, she thought. She had never been more surprised, but her breath came steady.

Her heart did not skip a beat. Alex really wanted to marry her, and there was a pleasant thrill in the knowledge. But the thrill was followed by a vague kind of sadness because she did not want to marry Alex.

She was fond of him, loved him in a way. But she was not in love with him and never would be.

CHAPTER 14

The previous evening had been merely the prologue to Anne's friendship with Barney Fosdick. That Sunday, at dinner, the real show began. A fine and very real friendship which, for so long as she lived, would be one of Anne's dearest memories.

He was waiting impatiently when they came, and to Anne's laughing surprise, the old man put his arms around her and kissed her. Then, holding her a little away from him, he tilted back her chin and studied her face thoughtfully. He said: "I've taken a great liking to you, my girl. Made up my mind about you the minute I saw you. You'd have suited me first rate for a daughter, if I'd ever had a girl of my own. Mind if I call you daughter?"

"Of course not," Anne said, smiling. "I think it would be nice."

Tonight he wore a wine red satin lounging robe. He looked every inch the handsome old actor as he handed them drinks—cocktails for himself and Alex, sherry for

Anne. Then he supervised the serving of the dinner which was wheeled in presently on a cart.

He was a sparkling conversationalist. Anne was entranced with his stories about his early days in Paris where, so he laughed, he might have got along faster with his art f he hadn't been so busy falling in love with a certain little French dancer. "Beautiful women were always my great weakness," he confessed, chuckling. One of the big troubles about growing old was that when a pretty young girl looked at him these days all she saw was a queer, eccentric old man.

"Now take you, daughter," he turned his bright eyes to Anne. "You think I'm a pretty odd old customer, don't you?"

Anne denied it instantly. "You shouldn't put words in my mouth, Barney." And she smiled. "I think you're a gifted artist, a fascinating man, and why do you refer to yourself as so old? You're not, really. Why?"

He sighed, shaking his head. "Because I feel old, daughter. Because I haven't much left but my dreams." And because the doctors had given him a very limited time to live. Then he apologized for bringing up such a depressing subject. But he wanted the two of them, Anne and Alex, to understand why he was having his luggage sent over here to Hillview. Why he had decided to stay here for several weeks. "I've taken a great fancy to you two. If I won't be an old nuisance and a bore,

I'd like to see a lot of you. We can dine together evenings, take some little trips together. Alex, my boy, could you arrange your office affairs so as to let me have Anne sometimes during the afternoons? She has a lovely voice, very restful, and my eyes have been troubling me. If she would care to take on the job of reading to me, I'd be delighted. Also I'd like a companion to take driving with me in the afternoons. I'm assuming I can rent a car. Now, in the fall, the woods are so lovely with the leaves beginning to turn, the promise of a long winter's sleep everywhere in nature, yet everything more beautiful than at any other season. I would pay you well, of course, daughter. I do not expect to get a charming and expert companion for nothing."

He gave her another of his warm, heart-moving smiles. "If I were thirty years younger, I would ask you to marry me. Since that is out of the question, I ask you to become my paid companion and protegé, and in return I shall leave you my fortune when I die."

Much of it was said in a half joking tone, and Anne took it as such. But Barney was perfectly serious about offering her a part-time job. In addition to other things, there was a lot of correspondence that needed to be attended to. And only a few days before, the doctor who had given him a checkup had suggested a nurse-companion. Someone who would provide congenial companionship, as well as being within call if he should need anyone.

"But I don't know a thing about nursing," Anne objected, although the suggested arrangement appealed to her surprisingly, possibly because she had already taken such a liking to the old artist. Laughing, she said: "While I don't imagine I'm indispensable in Alex's office, still it would put him in an awful humor to have someone else mixing up his files for him. He's learned how to find things when I mix them up."

"True, true," said Alex, grinning. "But I'll make a deal with you, Barney. I'll agree to share Anne with you, if you make a hard and fast promise, in writing, that I'm to get that painting of Anne when you get tired of it."

He had been willing, he said, to let Barney have *The Girl In A Yellow Scarf* on loan. But he didn't mean to let it get away from him completely.

Barney said that it would be arranged. And as to the nurse business: "Bah, daughter, what can a professional nurse do for me that you can't do? Except take my pulse and temperature, and those things I can do for myself."

There was, inevitably, talk—quite a lot of it—when the news got around that Anne Veigh had, first, quarreled with her mother and walked out of the house, and, second, was spending a great part of her time with Barney Fosdick as his paid companion.

Hillview, being a small obscure town where little ever happened in the way of excitement, was up to making quite a lot out of those two items.

Some of the talk was as ugly as it was absurd. "Nasty-minded old cats," was Aunt Molly's pronouncement, over the suggestion that Anne was thinking of marrying the old man. Because she was after his money? Or because she had changed, as sometimes happened to these "quiet girls," and turned into a little publicity hound?

Said Aunt Molly, with deepest scorn: "They just open their mouths and their tongues start wagging, and most of what comes out ought to be put with the garbage."

She said: "For heaven's sake, child, don't pay any attention to gossips, ever. Don't give them the satisfaction of even listening to their silly, lying jabber."

Anne didn't pay much attention, although she disliked the idea that unkind things were being said about that wonderful old man. She confided to Aunt Molly: "I'm as fond of him as if he were my own father. He's kind and generous and the most understanding person I've ever known. It's an education just to be with him and hear him talk. He's been to more places, known more important people, than anyone I've ever met. He's such a gifted artist, yet he never brags about it. He never brags about anything. And he's so lonely."

Thinking of that, the tears came. "It's so terribly sad,

Aunt Molly. A man who has had thousands of friends. He's had all sorts of medals and honors given him. He's given the world so much in his paintings. Yet now, when he's getting toward the end of his life, he has no one who seems to care anything about him. An apartment in New York with only a paid housekeeper in it. Now he's here in a strange little southern town with only Alex and me to fall back on. We can give him so little, I can do so little for him—read poetry to him, listen to him talk about the past, go for short drives with him. What does it amount to? Yet he's as grateful as if I were doing some big thing for him."

She was silent, thoughtful. When she spoke again, there was a quiet anger behind her words. "The town can talk its head off. It can have me in love with Barney Fosdick, trying to marry him to get his money, they can say any mean, lying thing they want to say about me. I shan't pay any attention to them. He's a sick, lonely man and, I think, the most wonderful man I ever knew. If there's any kindness I can do for him, I mean to do it. I know he hasn't long to live, and if I can make his last days less lonely, the town can gossip its head off. I intend to do what I can."

One night, toward the end of the third week of Barney's stay in Hillview, he was stricken with the most serious heart attack he had had yet. Kenny, who was called in, did what he could, doubting, however, that the old man would pull out of it. Barney did pull out of it, though. As soon as he was stronger, he announced that he wanted to get back to New York. There were things he must see to there. A few little business matters. He asked Anne to go along with him.

Anne put it up to Kenny, standing in the little sitting room in Barney's hotel suite. It was the first time she had seen Kenny to talk to in how long? Since the night of the party, she supposed. She had, however, heard talk. He had been seen several times in Eileen's company. It was, the town seemed to assume, just a matter of time until Eileen went to Reno and came back to make a formal announcement of her engagement to Kenny.

Poor Anne.

There were those willing to concede that you could scarcely blame poor Anne for her strange behavior of recent weeks. The way Kenny Wilcox had treated her—throwing her over because of Eileen's return. Since, naturally, it was assumed that Kenny had done the throwing over. It had hit her so hard, no doubt, that she had started kicking over the traces and went a little crazy. It happened that way, often, when a girl grieved so over some man who didn't want her.

There was a small bay window in the room. Anne stood in the little patch of sunlight that came through it, and found that her hands were very cold. Because it was late October and the real warmth gone out of the sun?

She said, watching Kenny walk across the small room toward her: "Barney would like me to go with him to New York. He says that I cheer him up and I believe that I do. Uncle Ned has a cousin with an apartment facing Central Park, a spinster with more rooms than she knows what to do with. I could stay with her. What do you think, Kenny? Would it do Barney any real good for me to tag along? Or would he be better off with a paid nurse, a stranger?"

His voice amazed her. It might have been a stranger speaking with marked malice. "Why ask me? I can tell you what his blood pressure is, and frankly it's dangerously high. I can tell you that the next time he has one of these attacks it will probably be the last one and that in the meantime he should have someone with him constantly. Preferably, in my opinion, a trained nurse. That's his angle. If the arrangement appeals to you as an interesting little adventure—a way of getting a little publicity for yourself by becoming the nurse-companion of a famous artist in his last days—then by all means go to it. You'll do him no harm. Since the old fellow seems to have taken a fancy to you, you might conceivably, from the psychological angle, be good for him. Cigarette?"

He took a pack out of his pocket and offered her one.

"No, thanks, Kenny." Anne shook her head slowly, staring at him with shocked eyes. She said quietly: "

knew that I was being talked about, with not one ounce of justification. But you, Kenny, accusing me of publicity seeking. How could you? You, who know me so well."

"I'm beginning to wonder if I know you at all," he said dully, and his eyes looked her up and down. "You've changed so much, Anne. You even look different."

In a way, she did, thanks to Barney's tactful suggestions that she pay a little more attention to lines and style that would bring out her own personality. She wore a moss green suit, severely plain except for the large buttons, the dashing cut of the collar. And with it a yellow scarf, worn largely to please Barney. He had ordered a dozen expensive scarfs for her, sent from one of New York's most expensive shops. Each of them either in basic yellow, or flaunting some charming pattern in yellow.

Anne decided that she would have a cigarette after all.

She stared at the lighted tip, without seeing it at all. She was only half aware that he had come very close to her. She was seeing another room on another afternoon not so long ago, hearing the muted richness in Kenny's voice saying to her: "I want to live here with you. . . And yet this other thing is like a madness in my blood, and until the madness is gone . . ."

She looked up suddenly, giving him her eyes fully.

"The madness won out, didn't it, Kenny? And I was right, after all. Because if I weren't right, if Eileen wasn't the winner, you would never, never in all this world, believe lying gossip about me." Her eyes held the aching hurt that had never really left her heart, and perhaps never would. Her lips were unsteady as she whispered: "Oh, Kenny." The very tone, tremulous, shaken, in which she spoke his name, was the measure of her love and of her helpless pain.

She had tried so hard to forget. I'll simply have to forget him, she had told herself over and over and over, since that afternoon when she had found him and Eileen together. The new interest which Barney's companionship had provided, some of the old man's wisdom so gently administered, had helped a little. It had helped her to imagine that she was beginning to get over it. But now the old longings, the intolerable emptiness and sense of loss, came back in a storm. I'll always love him, she thought, a little sick. There is no way of getting over it. No way at all.

Then anger was coming to her rescue, as Kenny said words as ridiculously untrue as they were unforgivable: "It was a clever little scheme, Anne, and I fell for it at the time." Kenny was deliberately nasty. "I was gullible enough to believe that you really were turning me down because of that old business with Eileen. It wasn't until later that I realized what a graceful out you had found for yourself."

His hands came down on her shoulders, rough and hurting her, and his eyes were stormy. "Oh, it was a slick idea, all right. You wanted to get out of our engagement because Alex Brooks had taken a fancy to you, and Alex had more to offer than I had. Then this old duffer with his weak heart came into the picture and offered bigger and broader horizons. Oh, I'm not accusing you of planning to marry the old relic as some people would have it. I don't believe you could bring yourself to do anything quite that ridiculous. But neither do I believe all this protegé business. That old exhibitionist, notorious for his past escapades wth women, squiring you around town. Driving you all around the country. Calling you daughter. By heaven, Anne, I can't understand the change in you. And now you're scheming to go off to New York with him and want me to back you up in it. Well, all I can say is, whatever it is you're after, I hope you get it. But don't expect me to aid and abet you in making a scandalous spectacle of yourself."

Spectacle of yourself. Eileen's words. So Anne knew. Knew as surely as that she breathed that it was Eileen who had been filling Kenny's ears with poison. It was done, before she knew that her hand had slapped his cheek smartly. "I hate you, Kenny Wilcox. Do you understand? I hate you." And for the moment she did.

"Do you?" Kenny said. Oddly, he seemed amused. Then, with no warning at all, his arms were around her. And for the moment, under his touch, at the feel of his mouth against her own, there was a singing in her ears, a blackness before her eyes, and her nails, dug into her palms, brought a physical reaction of pain of which she was completely unaware.

For the moment, the unforgivable indignity of his words was blanked out and there was only the wonder of being back home in his arms. Of being kissed as she had never been kissed before. Of being lost in his embrace, a girl without individuality and completely lost to herself.

Then: "Kiss me again, Anne. Let me kid myself a little longer."

"Kid yourself?" She was out of his arms, her eyes stormy again behind her wet lashes.

He said easily: "Sure. The way you just kissed me, I'd have sworn you were still my own love, if I didn't know better."

"What?" It was her tone, curt and ugly, that stopped him short. Then she laughed. "What a fool I am paying any attention to your barbed insults. Even listening to them. Speaking of malicious gossip, I might just as well tell you that I know exactly where you picked up all of your unkind remarks, because I heard them all first from Eileen. And speaking of kisses, I might remind you of a certain day that I walked into your office. And if you want me to believe that was a platonic embrace between you and Eileen, then I ask you just who is kidding whom?"

He said, quickly on the defensive, "I've always wanted to explain that, Anne. But you never gave me the chance."

"And I'm not giving you the chance now to feed me any pretty fairy stories. Anyway, why should you bother? Why don't you admit that you're still in love with Eileen—that it's Eileen you want—that it's simply a question of whether or not Eileen decides to divorce Bob? If it's any comfort to you, I think that she probably will, if for no other reason than that you'd be a change and Eileen, perpetually bored with too much sameness of anything, would do any rash thing for a new thrill."

He said flatly, with angry vehemence: "I have no idea of marrying Eileen. I don't know if she intends to divorce Bob, nor do I care. I've seen very little of her, and when I have seen her it's been more or less by accident. I have no interest in running around with another man's wife."

"And if she weren't another man's wife?"

He looked at her with subdued rage. Then, dully: "Why should I answer that question? You don't care anything about me, really. You've shown that plainly enough. First you ditched me, you've avoided me ever since, and now the first real chance we've had to talk, all you want to do is throw Eileen up to me. If you want my honest opinion, Anne, Eileen has proved a great convenience for you. Everything you want to get out of, you've used Eileen as an excuse. To get rid of me. To leave home. Now, no doubt, you'll manage to drag Eileen into it somehow as an excuse to get off to New York with your old Don Juan."

Anne said quickly: "Don't start dragging Barney Fosdick into this, Kenny. He's a grand person. His friendship has meant more to me than I could ever put into words. It's been both a privilege and an honor. He's given me a new outlook on life, and at the risk of having you laugh at me, I'll say that he's helped me to find myself. All of that Barney's friendship has meant to me. I won't stand for any slurs on that friendship."

"Very well. I apologize for taking this 'beautiful friendship' lightly. In my own defense—" there was a sudden change in his eyes, a surprising warmth— "may I suggest that a man eaten up with jealousy should be forgiven many things?"

"You?" Anne said, rather startled, but on the whole unbelieving. "Jealous of Barney Fosdick?" She laughed. "Oh, Kenny. Don't talk nonsense."

"Jealous of Barney," he said steadily. "Jealous of Alex Brooks. Jealous of that Ritter guy from Texas who dated you several times—to the vast annoyance of all of the other town gals. Just plain jealous. Don't you believe that, Anne?"

She thought, "If he's jealous, it's the dog in the manger variety."

Then he was saying, surprising her by the throbbing entreaty in his voice: "Anne, I don't want you to go off to New York. Old Fosdick can get someone else to go with him. I can find a nurse. Don't go, Anne. Please."

She looked up at him, a waiting look in her eyes, uncertainty in her heart. It was a long time before she answered him, and while she was silent, it was all up to him.

Had he taken her back into his arms, had he whispered: "Darling, I love you. I've found out that the madness for Eileen is over and done with. I've found out that it's you I want and only you and I love you so very, very much," she might have succumbed.

Would he, she wondered, as she waited, knowing that it would take only those few softly spoken words, only a certain look in his eyes, to bring her back to him in complete surrender??

Only so little and she would be ready to deliver over her heart to him, to have and to hold forever. Ready to promise: "Darling, from here on out, I shan't so much as move around the corner to the chain grocery, unless you want me to do it."

He did not say the words. Instead, mistaking her silence for stubborn refusal, he laughed shortly, not pleasantly.

Then, with a shrug: "Oh, well, you can't blame a guy for asking." His pat on her arm was as impersonal as if she had been a complete stranger, his tone equally impersonal.

"Well, have fun in New York, Anne."

"I haven't even said that I was going." It was as if her rebellious heart were still hoping for the words he had not spoken, although her eyes, empty now of everything except a curious quiet sadness, had given up hope.

He picked up his hat. "No. You haven't said you were going. But you will. I'd bet on that."

"What makes you so sure, Kenny?" Why couldn't he see that with a word he could stop her? Or didn't he want to stop her? That was it, of course. Fool that she was, quick to snatch up any scrap of tenderness thrown her way, she had managed to forget the unkind words he had pelted at her like hard pebbles dashed at her heart, managed to twist the more personal words into something he was far from meaning. "I don't want you to go." Probably that added up to nothing more than his male egotism. His vanity wanted the assurance that he still had enough hold on her to prevent her going. Many men were like that.

He stopped at the door, turning his face back to her as he considered her question. "What makes you so sure I will go?"

His words, finally, were not really an answer to anything. "There was a time, Anne, when I think you really wanted to go my way. You didn't wear a yellow scarf in those days. Now you are never seen without it. That's why I think you'll go to New York."

The door closed behind him. She stood for a while, feeling half sick. With the closing of the door, she felt as if something had died, quite finally. What had he been trying to tell her? About the scarf? That it was a sign she had changed, was no longer the same Anne as of old? That once the monotonous life as the wife of a small town doctor would have suited her, but now it was not enough? That now she wanted novelty and color and was after a kind of life that would offer them?

If that was it, he was wrong. Damnably wrong. She thought, her eyes swimming, Kenny is what I want. Perhaps later on, she would find other things to want—small, unimportant things which she would want in a small, unimportant way. But only because she had missed the one big thing that really mattered. And because a woman could not go on living unless she could find trivial things to want, even unimportant loves, to give a make-believe meaning to life.

She had not actually decided until that very moment to make the New York trip.

Now she thought: I might just as well go.

What was there to stay here for?

Indeed, how could she even bear to stay after the quiet, final closing of that door?

CHAPTER 15

New York was large and strange and, at first, a little terrifying. Even Uncle Ned's cousin Ella was something of a shock at their first meeting, largely because she was so different from what Anne had expected. A spinster?

The phrase was amusing, as applied to this handsome, stunningly dressed woman who had made a fortune in real estate before she was forty and who had not married simply because she couldn't see giving up her independence. "But don't you follow my wretched example, child," she advised Anne.

This career-woman business was, according to Ella, much overrated. True, you could dress beautifully, go and come as you pleased, without any worrisome bother of a husband and children who, according to legend, usually managed to break your heart, one way or another. But when all was said and done, a woman felt robbed, cheated of something when she had no one to break her heart over. It was a lonely business, facing old age with nothing but a nice bank account, an apartment full of furniture good for little except collecting dust, and the memory of the men you might have married, the children you might have had.

"You take my advice," said Cousin Ella, "and get a nice man. It's a girl's best bet."

Once the sense of strangeness had worn off, Anne found that she liked the woman enormously. Which was a good thing. Because as it turned out, much of her time was spent with Ella, who was delighted to have her as a guest, delighted to have someone to take shopping, to shows, to the more famous restaurants.

Barney Fosdick, who had taken an excited interest in the trip, began to fail rapidly as soon as he got back to New York. For the first week, a night nurse seemed sufficient and Anne spent much of the day with him.

The second week, however, the doctor ordered him to bed and insisted on a second nurse. Anne went in for an hour or so each afternoon, until even that seemed too much excitement for him.

He would fall asleep while she was reading to him. If she tried to make conversation, giving him her impressions of New York, he would smile and nod his head, but he seemed more intent on watching the changing expressions of her face. She guessed that it was a little too much effort for him to try to follow what she said.

She thought several times of returning to Hillview immediately. After all, what was the point in remaining in New York?

On the other hand, what was the point of her returning now that she was here?

What was there in Hillview for her?

Alex, fairly well satisfied now with a new secretary, would be just as well off without her. In fact, Anne doubted if she would want to return to his office. Too much of the personal had crept into their relationship. Just as well to let that drop and stay dropped. Alex had written her one note which had touched her deeply. "I love you, darling. Possibly because I'm something of an old rounder, it never seemed possible for me to say that to your face and make you understand that it was true. It is true. It's the first time in many years that it has been true for me. I just wanted you to know. The other thing that I want, very much, is for you to be happy. Always."

She had written him briefly in reply. "Thank you, Alex. Thank you so very, very much." What else was there to say, since the love that she had to give him in return was simply not enough? Some day, she hoped, they could return to being good friends.

Anne checked up on her bank balance, recalling that she had saved for years with the idea of treating herself to a nice trip one of these days. Why not make the most of it, now that she had the chance? She could afford some extravagances for once. Should she go into a shop and buy an expensive dress that struck her fancy? She could ride around in taxis, reveling in the feel of that small luxury without worrying about the small cost. She could insist on treating Cousin Ella to dinner occasionally, instead of having it always the other way around.

She said once, to the woman who had now become her staunch friend and confidante: "I've always been crazy to get to New York and I wonder if I didn't use dear Barney as an excuse to get here." She added, smiling: "I never had the spunk to just up and announce that I was going to do a certain thing because it appealed to me. Always had to have a good, logical excuse to make it seem a practical thing to do."

Ella sighed. "The things women cheat themselves out of because they grow up with the idea they shouldn't move or turn without a good reason for it." Life had taught her, she said, that the things you got the most fun out of were the things you did impulsively, with no rhyme or reason to them except that you wanted to do them.

She added, however, that she had been well along in years before she could afford the luxury of doing as she pleased.

"And I can't afford it for very long," Anne remembered worriedly. A few weeks of playing, going to shows, buying clothes she couldn't really afford, was all very well. But she had been wondering if there was any possibility of her getting a job in New York. Of course, office work was the only thing she knew anything about. And would she be any better off settling down to the monotonous drudgery of office work in New York, where living was so expensive?

She said doubtfully, and sensibly enough, "I suppose a lot of the glamour wears off, once a girl has to start riding the subway, living in a small room, watching every nickel and dime. I'd hate to burn all my bridges and then wish I hadn't."

"Stop worrying about it," Ella advised her briskly. "I have a notion, Anne, that you've always taken life a little too seriously. Now's a good time to allow yourself a breathing spell. You don't have to settle the course of your whole future life by breakfast tomorrow morning. Drift for a while. Drifting can be fun, and there's always the chance the little god of luck will give you a break you hadn't counted on."

"Luck." Anne had laughed. "I don't believe you ever trusted to luck, Cousin Ella. Not you. With all those real estate ventures."

"Luck played its part, at that. I recall one big deal—"

"Lady Luck is said to have her darlings," Anne said, her smile whimsical. "I've never been one of them."

"You must believe in luck, darling, if you expect it to do much for you." Ella was half laughing, half serious.

"You really think anything as intangible as luck could solve my immediate problems?" Anne looked definitely skeptical.

"I promise nothing, dear. I offer it as a possibility."

"Well, I won't bank on it," Anne said gaily. "I'm not the type to count on anything I don't work for and figure out for myself. I hope I'm wrong."

She was wrong.

A few nights later Barney Fosdick passed away in his sleep. When his will was made public, a few days later, the story was given considerable publicity. Everything that he owned was left to Anne.

His reputation as a great artist, one of the finest this country had produced, made his death an item of public interest. But it was Barney Fosdick's reputation as a Great Lover, his early marriage to a famous actress, the tradition of the score of women who had loved him madly—many of them famous beauties in their day—which warranted headlines appealing to the sensation-loving reading public.

And tied into every story of his so-called amorous past, featuring every headline was the story of the unknown girl from the unknown little southern town who had been with him in his last hours. The girl who had accompanied him to New York and rarely left his bedside—to whom he had left everything that he owned.

Anne Veigh. *The Girl In The Yellow Scarf.* Th

painting was discovered, reproduced with every story. The words became a kind of by-line appearing under pictures of Anne in papers all over the country. An enterprising song writer set immediately to work creating a song to go with the title. Who is Anne Veigh? Barney Fosdick's protégé, as he had called her, or his last great love? That was the question everyone asked.

Anne, deeply grieved over her friend's death, was furious and practically helpless against the first bewildering assault of the reporters. "What shall I tell them?" he asked Ella, who advised her wisely: "Just look sweet and charming and tell them as little as possible. Just give them a few leads; then let them make what they want out of it. If you make them like you, they'll doubtless write up some very flattering fairy stories. If you antagonize them, they'll make you appear an unpleasant little adventuress. Personally, I've found it a sensible thing to make reporters like me. Nor can I see any reason to get upset because they hound you. After all, a reporter is only another human being with a job to do and worried about losing it, like anyone else. Don't look so upset, Anne dear. This may prove a very good thing for you. This may be the knock of Lady Luck, just as I predicted."

Anne laughed shortly. "Luck? Losing the dearest friend I ever had. And as for Barney's so-called fortune, that's just a myth. I've talked with his lawyers. About all he left were debts."

"I know, dear," Cousin Ella said calmly. "I didn't imagine that Barney had any fortune to leave. It's been years since he did much painting and his kind usually die broke. But money isn't everything. There are other kinds of luck. This whole thing will bring you before the public eye. You may get something big out of it. Possibly the offer of a good job."

The offers started coming almost immediately. Amazingly flattering, until Anne stopped to consider that she had done nothing to earn or even deserve them. Was this one of the ways in which girls slid up to fame and the good places? A lucky break; a few headlines spread across a newspaper; a tag line, *The Yellow Scarf Girl,* identifying her with a color and gaiety of personality which, in fact, she had never possessed?

Finally came the most surprising offer of all from one of New York's largest, if not the largest, advertising agency. She was, they thought, the very model they had been looking for. The salary they offered was, to Anne's conservative way of thinking, fabulous. And inevitably the thought came to her as she read the letter making her the offer: Eileen would have given her right eye to be a New York model.

But that lovely plum had fallen to Anne. She laughed thinking about that, with a feeling of small but certainly justified triumph. Then came the sobering thought

stripping even this achievement of much of its thrill:
But Eileen can have what I really want. Kenny.

"I think," she told Cousin Ella, "that I'd better make
a trip home before I decide definitely."

After all, if only as a matter of respect, she should
talk it over with her mother before committing her
future, possibly for years to come.

"And of course," said her friend, "you should talk it
over with the young man."

"There isn't any young man," Anne said, curiously
irritated. "There was once. But that's all over."

Was it over? A hundred times, maybe a thousand
times, Anne had gone over that last meeting with Kenny.
Recalling things he had said, wondering about possible
implicatons behind his words. Could it possibly be that
he had been trying to tell her that he still loved her, but
had been too proud to say it in so many words? Maybe
he was even afraid to say it. She had never been able to
get rid of the nagging uncertainty. She had never been
able to make up her mind for sure. But after her trip
home she would be sure.

CHAPTER 16

A gentle snow was falling, still little more than a mist
as Anne got off the train that morning. Surprisingly
she felt a real thrill as the station taxi drove her up to
the house and she got out, wondering what kind of a
reception she would receive. She had thought of wiring
ahead that she was coming, then changed her mind.

It was a Sunday, still fairly early, and Nellie and
Eileen were at breakfast. "Hello, darlings," Anne said
gaily, walking into the kitchen, which looked cheerful
and cozy with the snow misting the window panes. "Is
there an extra cup of coffee for the prodigal daughter?"
Then Nellie had Anne in her arms, was laughing and
crying both at once. "Anne, Anne, it's so good to see
you. You wrote so little. So much seems to have been
happening to you, but we had to read most of it in the
paper. Anne, you're thin. Too much flying around, I
guess, and not eating properly. What you need is some
good home cooking."

It was genuine and heart-warming, and Anne

thought, amazed, Why, Mother is really glad to see me. Had her own feeling in the past that she was being slighted been largely her imagination?

Eileen said: "Hello, Anne. You seem to have had quite a time for yourself, inheriting fortunes and hitting the front pages." But there was no malice in the words, and although she managed a smile, Anne noticed that Eileen's eyes looked reddened as if she had been crying.

After she had poured Anne a cup of coffee, Nellie explained: "Eileen has had some bad news. Bob has been in an accident. She thinks she must go to him."

Eileen finished her breakfast and got up. "Mother, I know you have a thousand questions to ask Anne, but you'll have her to yourself later. Mind if I take her upstairs while I pack?"

Up in her room, Eileen broke completely. Anne thought, watching, "It's the first time I've ever seen her weep genuine, unashamed tears, not the variety turned on for effect." She said gently, greatly moved: "Don't sis. Please don't cry that way. Why should you? It isn't as if Bob were fatally injured. A broken arm and a few cracked ribs can be mended."

"He might have been killed! That's what I keep thinking about. That, and what a mess I am. You told me once that I ought to grow up, and you were right. You must detest the sight of my face, and if you don't you ought to. I'm mean and spoiled and selfish. I always have been. Bob knew that before I left him. I'm not even sure that he wants me back. But I'm going to try to make him want me. I'm going to try to grow up and deserve him. I've got to try. Do you think I can make it, Anne? Do you?"

"Of course you can, darling. Don't talk nonsense. There's nothing wrong with you. Only that you were always so darned beautiful and glamorous, and people made a fuss over you, and you aren't to blame for that. Here, blow." And she handed Eileen a handkerchief.

Then, as another thought struck her, Anne said soberly: "What about Kenny?"

Eileen. who had thrown herself over the bed, sat up, dabbing at her eyes. "Well, what about him?"

Anne said: "I'm asking you. Does he know that you're going back to Bob? Won't it hit him a pretty hard blow?" She added, not too gently: "You hurt Kenny once before. If you're doing it again—"

Eileen looked amazed for a moment; then she laughed. "I keep forgetting what an innocent you still are in some ways. Haven't you realized yet that Kenny Wilcox doesn't give a hoot about me? He made that clear enough from the very day I came home."

Then, seeing Anne's wide-eyed look of disbelief: "Listen, Anne, and this is the truth, believe me. Kenny is yours if you want him. Since this is my confession hour, I'll admit that I came home with the idea of bringing the lad to my feet again. Just one of my nasty little ways. I couldn't bear the idea that he had got over his old infatuation for me. I made a play for him and got turned down cold. I think he rather disliked me."

"But that day in his office, Eileen—"

"Oh, yes. That day in his office, when you caught us in the life and death clinch." And Eileen laughed shortly. "Well, that was just little Eileen up to some more of her cute tricks. It isn't impossible, you know, for a girl to *make* a man make a little love to her. There are ways and methods and I know them all. I've been telling you,' she said harshly, "that I'm a detestable kind of person.

"And I'm at my best, when it comes to meanness, when I get turned down. You know the old corn about the woman scorned. Well, that day I found out, and no fooling, that Kenny wanted no part of me. I couldn't take it without getting even with both of you. Remember, I didn't really want Kenny. For what my love is worth, it belongs to Bob, but I wanted the satisfaction of knowing I could take Kenny over if I had wanted him. If I couldn't, I was determined that you shouldn't have him."

Anne said slowly, as the picture began to come clear: "So you filled Kenny's head with a lot of wrong ideas about me. You made him believe I'd turned man-crazy and became a little publicity hound as well."

"Don't start scolding," Eileen said a little crossly as she got out her bags and started to pack. "I'm admitting I'm a little stinker. I'm not asking you to be noble and forgive all at the drop of a hat. But I can't stand having you rub it in, either. Right this minute, I'm busy enough hating myself. I don't want to hear how much you hate me."

"I don't hate you, sis," Anne said quietly, getting up. "I just want to get all this straight."

Eileen paused in the process of folding an evening dress. She looked at Anne and asked bluntly: "Do you still want him? Remember, I don't know what's in your mind. You wrote that you were taking a job as a model."

Anne said, completely indifferent: "I can have the job if I want it."

"But you'd rather have Kenny? Then for heaven's sake, go and grab him and put the poor guy out of his misery. He's lost about twenty pounds, his eyes are sunken, most of his patients are worrying that they're going to lose their favorite doctor. He's a horrible example of what unrequited love can do to an otherwise sensible man. And if you don't believe me, just go and ask him. Just ask him."

Ask him? How? How did a girl go about asking a man to take her in his arms and hold her there forever? How could she ask him to whisper, "I love you, darling," when there was always the chance, her pride reminded her, that he didn't? When all that he did was seat her across an office desk, then seat himself, light a cigarette, start asking her questions about a dozen things that didn't matter, and all in a voice so painfully polite that she could have screamed.

She had phoned him, arranged at her own suggestion to meet him at his office. And now here she was, facing his cool smile, his perfectly controlled face, and wondering, horrified, if Eileen, in her upset, almost hysterical state of mind, had misrepresented everything.

"You're looking fine," Kenny said, adding with a touch of sarcasm, "You seem to have cut quite a dash in New York."

She resented that. "I lost a dear friend, Kenny." Her tone a rebuke. "I wish you could have known Barney. Then you would understand what I mean when I say that he was a very wonderful person. The papers gave such a false picture of him."

He was quickly apologetic. "I didn't mean that the way it sounded, Anne. I was thinking of all the publicity, which I suppose any girl would find rather exciting."

"Naturally," she said, her tone perfectly calm, the suggestion of a dangerous gleam in her eye. "I remember so well how you accused me of being after publicity. So if you were right, I got what I was after, didn't I?"

Kenny had the grace to flush embarrassedly. "I didn't say quite that, Anne."

"You said exactly that. It was one of the very last things you did say to me, and I've thought of it often."

"Well, when a girl starts doing things to attract attention—running off from home, dropping old friends, forming a new friendship which can't help but be conspicuous, if only because the man is well known, what should people think? I see you still go in for yellow scarfs," he finished absurdly.

They were quarreling, glowering at each other like two kids.

Anne touched the soft silk at her throat which went beautifully with the rich brown of her suede suit. "I'm still wearing a yellow scarf," she said coolly. "Perhaps I always shall. It has brought me, helped to bring me, something I never had before." She was thinking in terms of the richness of a friendship and of a self-understanding and confidence in herself which had come from that friendship.

Kenny, misinterpreting her meaning, said quickly: "Yes. I see what you mean. It played its part in bringing you a fortune, didn't it?"

Anne didn't understand him at first. When she did, she smiled. "A fortune that didn't exist. Barney had no fortune to leave to anyone, if that's what you're getting at. But it made a good newspaper story, didn't it?"

She said in a small voice: "Would you have been more interested in me if I had come home an heiress?"

There was a pause before he said, smiling a trifle: "That question strikes me as a little too silly to answer. However, if the legacy was just a false alarm, I'm sorry, for your sake."

"Oh, don't feel sorry for me, Kenny. I'm doing all right. I have a lovely job as a model offered me. I'll probably take it, since there seems to be nothing more promising on the horizon."

She stood up suddenly. "Well, Kenny, it's been nice seeing you again. I'll probably be around for a week or two. Drop over and see me if you have a spare moment."

"Thanks. I'll do that.'

She was almost to the door when her composure left her. Suddenly she turned, and her lashes were wet: "Did you have to be so darned polite about everything? Couldn't you have acted just a little human?"

Then she saw him move, like a swift, graceful animal. Then she felt his arms and heard his voice. "What are you saying, Anne What are you trying to tell me?"

"You know. You must know. If you don't, you're just plain stupid." Then she was crying without shame. A storm of tears, sobs in her throat, her head on his shoulder. She whispered brokenly: "I'm throwing myself at you, and I never thought I'd do that with any man, but I've got to know where I stand. I've got to know. We had so much once, Kenny—so very much. I tossed it all away, and I've never known whether it was an awful mistake. If you don't want me any more, all you have to do is say so and I'll never bother you again, but I've got to know. I've just got to know for sure."

His voice was gentle and he was actually on his knees to her. He held her close, and her hand, touching his cheek, found the unashamed tears on it. "You're the one who's stupid, my darling, if you don't know how I feel about you. I tried to tell you, that last day—tried to make you understand that I still loved you, wanted you."

"Is that what you were trying to tell me?" She heard her own laughter, a little out of control. "Then why didn't you say so? A man doesn't usually make an avowal of love by heaping insults on the girl of his heart."

He reminded her soberly: "I never intended to insult you, but I told you I was jealous, and I was. Eaten up with it. You seemed to have changed so, and how was I to know but what your feeling for me had changed? After all, my darling, you were the one who broke things off. Just don't forget that."

"You knew why I did it. Eileen."

"Oh, the devil with Eileen. I'm allergic to that name. Eileen was the reason you gave, but—"

"But you didn't know how you'd feel when you saw

her again. You told me that, Kenny. You said over and over that you just didn't know."

"Yes," harshly. "And when I did know, you never gave me a chance to tell you about it. You deliberately avoided me."

He stood up, gathering her wholly into his arms. "Oh, does it matter what I said and you said?" He had found her lips, and for a moment the only sound Anne heard was the ecstatic song in her own heart.

Then he released her partly, just enough to tilt her chin and look deeply into her eyes. "Let's just say that between us, we made a complete hash of everything. And maybe it was a good thing. Losing you taught me how very dear you are to me. Oh, Anne, Anne, nothing was any good without you. Nothing. Tell me just this one thing, darling. Tell me that this is real. Your coming back to me, your being here in my arms. Tell me I won't wake up and discover I've been dreaming. Tell me that you love me."

Softly, with the rapture of a girl in love in her voice, she whispered the words: "You aren't dreaming, darling. And you are my love. My only love. You always will be."

Satisfied for a moment, he caught her back to him. Then, suddenly jealous, he asked her: "What about that modeling job?"

"Well, what about it, Kenny?"

"Sure you haven't any doubts about turning it down? That kind of job is the sort of thing a million girls dream about, isn't it?"

Anne laughed. "Oh, Kenny, darling. The things you don't know about women. Hasn't anyone ever told you why a girl wants to go to New York and become a model? Simply because it's a highly thought of method of getting a man. Me, darling, I seem to have landed my man!"

Kenny grinned, then kissed her. It was a kiss that told her he was hers for now and for always.